BRIDGE AT THE ENIGMA CLUB

PETER WINKLER

FOREWORD BY CHIP MARTEL

MASTER POINT PRESS • TORONTO, CANADA

Master Point Press
331 Douglas Ave.
Toronto, Ontario, Canada
M5M 1H2   (416) 781-0351

Email: info@masterpointpress.com

Websites: www.masterpointpress.com
                   www.teachbridge.com
                   www.bridgeblogging.com
                   www.ebooksbridge.com

Library and Archives Canada Cataloguing in Publication

Winkler, P. (Peter), 1946-
          Bridge at the Enigma Club / Peter Winkler.

Includes bibliographical references.

          1. Contract bridge–Fiction. I. Title.

PS3623.I553B75 2010   813'.6   C2010-902903-8

Editor   Ray Lee
Copy editor/interior format   Sally Sparrow
Cover and interior design   Olena S. Sullivan/New Mediatrix

2 3 4 5 6 7   18 17 16 15

What you hold in your hand is no ordinary bridge book. True, it tells an entertaining story that features colorful characters and fascinating deals—some from actual play, some the likes of which you have never seen before.

But this book also introduces a host of new ideas for bidding and defense, while giving you a glimpse into a possible computerized future for bridge.

And, importantly, it is the first and only book in the world about cryptologic methods in bridge: learn to (legally) communicate in secret with your bridge partner. You can show your controls while your opponents languish in the dark; and you can signal on defense without telling declarer how to play the hand.

You don't believe it? Neither does 'Tush' Tischman, intrepid hero of *Bridge at the Enigma Club*, until he becomes the victim. Poor Tush, lured by a pretty girl into a bridge club like no other. Luckily it is he, and not you, who must suffer while you laugh (and learn).

Here you will see more new ideas in bridge than you ever dreamed of. Will you agree with all of them? Probably not (I don't). And some of the suggested systems and conventions are not permitted in your local game or tournament, at least for now. But whether you love Winkler's ideas or (like Tush) are totally outraged, you can't fail to enjoy this one-of-a-kind volume.

So, read and enjoy. Chances are, you'll never look at bridge quite the same way again.

Chip Martel, April 2010

BRIDGE AT THE ENIGMA CLUB

Corky, wherever you are... please forgive me. I know I
messed up, but until then we were good together, don't you
think? Let's play again sometime.

Robert

She stood dripping against the carved facade of a ten-story building, make-up smeared, curls ruined, eyes defiant—in short, irresistible. In her fist, as if he had willed it there himself, was the soggy but unmistakable corpus of an ACBL convention card.

"Get stood up by your partner?"

A compression of the lips was sufficient answer.

"Perhaps I can offer myself as a substitute."

"You wouldn't want to play with someone in my frame of mind."

"I'll take my chances," he said offhandedly. "I'm a good player, and I can adapt. I just finished a business meeting, but I don't fly home until tomorrow. Where's the game?"

She paused, looked him over, and sighed. "Follow me."

He tried to look casual, but his heart raced; a minute ago he'd been taking a bored, aimless walk in an unfamiliar city. Now, suddenly, an afternoon of bridge! True, his partner was unknown and unhappy. But he knew he could change that.

X X X

Robert 'Tush' Tischman was a Nice Guy and, indeed, a fine bridge player. He was good at many things, in fact, when he concentrated— but at times he had trouble doing that, and allowed his emotions to get the better of him.

He had acquired the nickname 'Tush' (rhymes with bush) on account of some childhood pudginess, combined with the lure of alliteration. Now a young man, he was in fact quite presentable, if at times a bit earnest. Unmarried but looking around, he often dreamed that he could find a girl he could love and play bridge with. Alas, young female bridge players seemed to be a rare commodity in the twenty-first century.

Tush understood that his wet and angry companion in the elevator might be a poor bridge player, and, moreover, might be attached or even married (though her ring finger was bare). At least she was *willing* to play—with someone. But wasn't he getting ahead of himself?

Concentrate! Play a solid, strong game, he told himself, and behave.
Be a good partner. Impress this young woman. Then, what happens,
happens.

What happened next, in fact, was that the elevator doors opened to
reveal a slightly decrepit art-deco hallway from which emanated a maze
of smallish rooms. Several "Hi, Corky" greetings were directed toward
Tush's partner, but she seemed in no mood to respond. She led Tush
to a room with only one table in it, and saying "I'd better sit North to
score," she indicated the South seat for Tush.

In contrast to its seventy-five-year-old surroundings, the table itself
was a high-tech affair. Tush saw that built into the table surface in front
of each player was a private touch screen. 'Corky' did something on
hers and a list of systems appeared before Tush:

```
YELLOW CARD
2/1
PRECISION
RICOCHET
OTHER
```

"We don't have time to put in details," said Corky brusquely. "What's
your poison?"

"Um, I guess Standard American Yellow Card will have to do."

TUSH LEARNS THE ROPES

As Tush pushed the yellow card button on his touch screen, a gangly middle-aged fellow and a demure-looking elderly woman—his mother, perhaps?—appeared and sat themselves East and West, respectively.

"Ay, Corky!" said the guy. "Who's your partner?"

"Beats me. I just found him on the street."

"Robert," said Tush, quickly sticking out his hand. "Good to meet you, and you too" (this to the woman).

"I'm George, this is Tricia," said East, while his partner fumbled in her pocketbook, finally extracting a convention card. This she inserted into a slot in the table; it was regurgitated with a soft acknowledging "beep." Tush could see that the card itself was a computer printout, and had bar codes as well as human-readable convention information.

"I take it that East-West pairs enter their convention cards before each round?"

"My goodness, no," said Tricia. "The tables communicate. Are you ready to begin?"

Tush nodded and Corky pushed a button. With a whirring sound, cards began to appear in a slot in front of Tush. He must have looked a bit startled, because West (Tricia) said sweetly, "I take it you're not used to real-time computer dealing, Robert?"

Tush smiled pleasantly, reluctant to acknowledge that this old lady was more technologically savvy than he. As he picked up his cards he noted that, indeed, they were also bar-coded. Hmm, that meant the cards could be freshly dealt at each table—no chance for misdeals caused by putting the cards back incorrectly. Come to think of it, they could even play the same deals simultaneously at every table—perhaps they were.

Holding:

♠A 5 4 2   ♡Q 7   ◇6   ♣A 7 6 5 3 2

and thinking that this was worth an opening bid, Tush looked up to see if he was the dealer. On the table before him words appeared:

```
BOARD 1
DEALER NORTH
NONE VUL
```

It occurred to Tush that since they were at Table 7, yet beginning with
Board 1, they probably *were* playing Board 1 everywhere at the same
time. Tush looked down again, this time seeing:

```
WEST        NORTH       EAST        SOUTH
            1NT
```

So Corky had opened one notrump, presumably by pushing a button
on her own touch screen. After a moment the display changed again:

```
WEST        NORTH       EAST        SOUTH
            1NT         2♠
                        (NATURAL)
```

Pretty cool, thought Tush. It tells you what the opponents bids mean;
you don't have to ask. Presumably the opponents were told "15–17
HCP" after Corky's opening. Looking down at the display, Tush saw
that he had not yet even been offered an option; the computer was
doing a mandatory countdown while the words:

```
WAIT—OPPONENTS HAVE INTERFERED
```

appeared on the screen. After ten seconds a bidding option display
appeared before Tush:

```
PASS  DOUBLE
2    3    4    5    6    7
♣   ◇   ♡   ♠   NT
```

Tush noted that one-level bids and redouble were not presented to him as options. Presumably, it wouldn't even allow him to bid, say, two clubs. No chance of an insufficient bid. Or a bid out of turn. Not to mention a bid without appropriate hesitation.

What, indeed, *should* he bid? In a moment of panic, he thought, oh my god, is Lebensohl on the Yellow Card? If so, fast or slow? No, surely not. Whew. Double would be business, too, probably, but this hand was an obvious 3NT call.

Looking down at the screen, he pushed "3" then "NT" and was gratified to see the updated bidding display:

```
WEST        NORTH       EAST        SOUTH
            1NT         2♠          3NT
```

which, a few seconds later, had been augmented to:

```
WEST        NORTH       EAST        SOUTH
            1NT         2♠          3NT
ALL PASS
```

and then:

```
CONTRACT: 3NT BY NORTH
```

East looked down at his table display, no doubt seeing something like:

```
YOUR LEAD
```

and put the ♠K on the table.

Tush put down his dummy and, rather impolitely, peeked into his opponents' hands, mentally reconstructing his partner's.

Contract: 3NT by North
Opening lead: ♠K

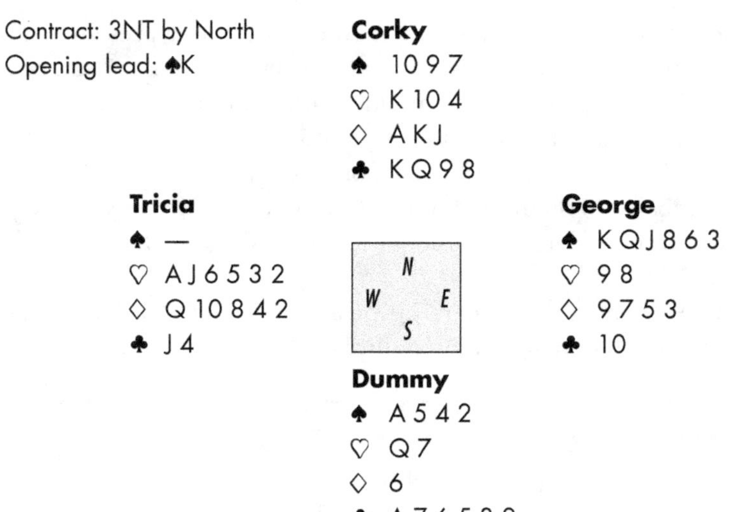

Corky
♠ 10 9 7
♡ K 10 4
◇ A K J
♣ K Q 9 8

Tricia
♠ —
♡ A J 6 5 3 2
◇ Q 10 8 4 2
♣ J 4

George
♠ K Q J 8 6 3
♡ 9 8
◇ 9 7 5 3
♣ 10

Dummy
♠ A 5 4 2
♡ Q 7
◇ 6
♣ A 7 6 5 3 2

Tush counted ten top tricks: a spade, a heart, two diamonds and six clubs. A diamond finesse would make eleven. The heart finesse, available on an endplay if the clubs were run first, would make it twelve. Plus 490 would be a nice way to start.

However, Corky ducked the opening lead in dummy.

Plus 460, thought Tush.

East continued with the ♠J, and Corky ducked again.

Oh well, 430.

East persisted with the ♠Q, and Corky ducked again!

Would you believe 400?

West had pitched the ♡6, ♡2 and ♡3 on the first three tricks, and now East switched to a heart to her ace. Corky claimed the remainder, explaining that she would play the ♣K, ♣Q and ♣A and then unblock her ♣9 under dummy's ♠A.

"Very nice safety play," said Tush, trying not to sound condescending, "but was that the percentage line? Clubs'll break 2-1 more than seventy-five percent of the time, and even if they don't, you still may make the contract. Those overtricks can be valuable."

"Actually, they're worthless, by my reckoning," said East. "You're down 11 IMPs regardless."

"What!?"

"We play IMPs against par here," said Corky, her tone suggesting that anything else was passé.

Tush looked at the table screen. The full deal was displayed in front of each player, along with the following information:

```
PAR: 6NT BY NORTH OR SOUTH, N-S +990
CONTRACT: 3NT BY NORTH, MAKING 3
RESULT: +400 N-S
DIFFERENCE -590 = -11 IMPS
```

"Are you kidding me?" said Tush, outraged. "Nobody can get to slam! We're getting charged eleven IMPs for this?"

"Relax," said Corky. "All the other North-South pairs will lose eleven IMPs on this deal, too, and in the end, our IMP scores are compared only with pairs who play in the same direction we do."

Tush took a deep breath. "Okay, okay, I guess if everyone plays this deal, it's fair. But really, you're comparing people to double-dummy par? Does that make any sense? What's wrong with matchpoints, anyway?"

George peered at Tush. "Matchpoints? Are you serious? What an awful game! Just think, good bridge like your partner just showed us would go to waste. Nobody likes matchpoints any more. Do you ever see a bridge column about a matchpoint deal? Of course not! The whole idea of *contract* bridge is that you're supposed to concentrate on making your contract. Games and slams are supposed to be more important than partials. Matchpoints! Yuck!"

"Now, George, dear," Tricia soothed, "let's not go overboard. You used to play matchpoints yourself, once upon a time. It can have its charms. And with the old technology, it made some sense: every deal had the same amount of time allotted to it, so it was natural to have the same number of points available for each board, whether it be partscore or slam, and whether it be flat or exciting. Now that we can all play the boards at the same time, the director can call the round whenever he wants, and we have the time we need to work out a trump squeeze. With matchpoints, you have a different outlook."

"Yeah, but you notice people at tournaments are playing fewer and fewer pairs games and more and more teams—except for those IMP pairs. I'm telling you, matchpoints is on its way out."

"Since you mentioned IMP pairs," interjected Tush, "don't they calculate some sort of median score to compare against? I mean, I've never heard of IMPing against double-dummy par. Mightn't that be a bit weird? Take this deal, for example. If some North-South pair stops in two notrump, they'd lose—let's see—thirteen IMPs, only two more than the game bidders."

"True," said George, "you do get a few oddities like that, but it evens out in the end. Anyway, the advantages more than outweigh the occasional oddball score. For example, the same result gets the same score, no matter when or where in the world the deal comes up. And you get to find out that score on the spot."

"If you ask me," Tricia contributed, "the biggest advantage is that it's more fun. You find out at the end of the deal what could have been made, and often that's quite eye-opening. Fancy plays you didn't see, sacrifices you missed… and at this club, you usually have time to discuss the hands after each round."

It did occur to Tush that with modern bridge software, it was a cinch now to compute double-dummy par, and he imagined the results could be entertaining.

"You do play IMPs against par at home, don't you, Robert?" asked Tricia. "When you've only got one table? It was a drag in the old days keeping total points, it was always just a matter of who got the best cards."

"Um, I can see the advantages, but without the computer, how do you know what's par?"

"You work it out—that's half the fun. If there's a dispute, you change hands and play it through with the cards face up."

"Switch hands? What for?"

"Well, suppose I go down in four spades, and I claim it was unmakeable, par should be +140. But you argue that it could have been made. No problem, we pass hands to the left and you try to make it while we defend. It's like the famous story about the slow camels."

Even Corky looked mystified at this reference.

"Two nomads meet in the desert, each complaining about how slow his camel is. Trying to outdo each other's complaints, they make a bet—I don't know, 100 pieces of silver?—and organize a race. Whoever is last to get to the finish, wins.

"Naturally each nomad holds his camel back until they both stop, and it's obvious the race will never finish. Finally a third nomad comes by with a suggestion: switch camels!"

While Tush pondered the camel analogy, another thought entered his head. "Getting back to this club," he said, "when average on a deal could be anything, it must be difficult to make score adjustments when there are irregularities."

"What irregularities?" said George. "The table won't let us make an illegal bid, incorrect explanations are rare, unauthorized information obviated, misdeals impossible. We hardly ever see the director. And, of course, with all deals played simultaneously, it's easy to design the movement so that everyone plays all the deals."

"Don't you ever have a sit-out? What if an odd number of pairs show up?"

"No problem, we put in two computers as one of the stationary pairs."

"And the occasional revoke? That must happen, right? I mean, you haven't gone to electronic cards."

"True," said Tricia. "Some people still insist that they like the feel of real plastic in their hands." Clearly, Tricia did not count herself among these fuddy-duddies. "But if there's a revoke, no problem, P-G follows the ACBL rules, and if a result has to be second-guessed, he just calculates the new IMP result."

"P-G is our director and founder," Corky explained. "You'll get to meet him later."

Tush nodded. "Must be an interesting person," he said, but he was occupied with pleasant thoughts about what lay ahead for the afternoon. True, this club seemed to be a little unusual, but they knew how to play. In particular, his partner had immediately spotted the club blockage and found a 100% line to make the contract. (If West had switched to a red suit earlier, it would have given Corky her ninth trick; after a passive club exit, if East had shown out, she could have just continued spades herself.) She was attractive, and smart. Not as smart as Tush, perhaps, but who was? If he could impress her, get to know her better, who knew what could come of it.

TUSH SHOWS OFF AS DECLARER

Second to speak with

♠ A Q 4   ♡ A 6 5 4 2   ◇ J 6 3   ♣ 10 3

Tush ventured a scrawny 1♡ opener. Tricia overcalled 1♠, Corky doubled, and after George passed Tush bid the obvious 1NT, ending the auction.

West	North	East	South
Tricia	Corky	George	Tush
		pass	1♡
1♠	dbl	pass	1NT
all pass			

The ◇4 was led and when dummy came down, Tush saw that he was in a precarious contract—the kind of thing that can easily happen when both partners stretch.

Contract: 1NT by South
Opening lead: ◇4

Dummy
♠ 10 7 3
♡ Q 3
◇ K 10 5
♣ K J 8 5 4

Tush
♠ A Q 4
♡ A 6 5 4 2
◇ J 6 3
♣ 10 3

Tush played low from dummy; East won the ace and returned the ♠8, covered by the ♠Q and ♠K. West switched back to the ◇7, won in dummy with the ten.

Tush had been thinking, and now smoothly led a club from dummy, knowing that it would be hard for East to climb up second in hand with the queen. Surprise, surprise: Tush's ten held the trick! Hmm, thought Tush happily, West must be holding ♣Axx and playing declarer for Q10x. Tush led another club to the board's king, again holding the trick.

Suddenly, Tush was in overtrick land: the ♣A and ♣Q could surely now be crashed, and that meant eight tricks for declarer: a spade, a heart, two diamonds and four clubs.

The complete deal was:

Dummy
- ♠ 10 7 3
- ♡ Q 3
- ◇ K 10 5
- ♣ K J 8 5 4

Tricia
- ♠ K J 9 5 2
- ♡ 10
- ◇ Q 9 7 4
- ♣ A 7 2

George
- ♠ 8 6
- ♡ K J 9 8 7
- ◇ A 8 2
- ♣ Q 9 6

Tush
- ♠ A Q 4
- ♡ A 6 5 4 2
- ◇ J 6 3
- ♣ 10 3

This was the position after Trick five:

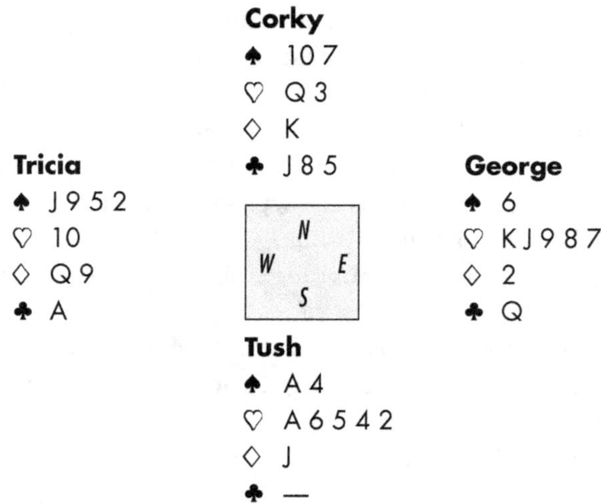

In the back of his mind, Tush had been accumulating a picture of West's hand: five spades, apparently four diamonds, three clubs and thus a stiff heart. If this was really so, he could wring yet another trick out of this layout.

Backing his judgment to the hilt, Tush cashed the ♡A and ◇K, setting up five tricks for the defense and burning his entry to the dummy. *Then* he gave up the club.

In with the ♣A, West could cash the thirteenth diamond but then had to give declarer both a second spade trick and a new entry to the good clubs on the board. Making three!

Par was +120 by East-West for 2NT—7 fat IMPs to Tush and Corky.

"I guess I should have played my queen of clubs on the first round," said George ruefully.

Tricia sighed. "I had a few chances to beat this, as well. Nicely done by Robert, here."

Tush glowed. It was an auspicious start, for sure.

TUSH TIPS OFF THE LEAD

Two portly men approached and sat East-West, neither offering an introduction. They picked up their hands; Corky and Tush did the same.

Tush peered at

♠ K Q 9 6 4   ♡ J 8 3   ◇ A K J 7 2   ♣ —

an agreeable collection. He opened 1♠ as dealer and was delighted to see Corky's response of 2NT, Jacoby, showing a forcing spade raise.

Now what? Opener's rebid of 3♣ would show shortness, but Tush remembered that a jump to the four-level is used to show a good five-card side suit. And there was also that other issue: should he be trying to bid this hand scientifically at all? Maybe he should just bid 6♠, and not tip off the opponents to the possibly deadly heart lead.

Trouble was, this hand could belong in a *grand*. Worse, he was trying to be a good partner, and really should put Corky in the picture. The bid that did that was 4◇. In fact, Tush felt that the hand really *wanted* to bid 4◇. So he let it.

Partner's 5♣ reply was a disappointment, but at least it made for a cogent auction. Tush bid 5♠ knowing that if partner had second-round heart control, she would bid the slam—perhaps in notrump, if she had the ♡K.

That was the end of the auction, though. The bidding had been:

West	North	East	South
			1♠
pass	2NT	pass	4◇
pass	5♣	pass	5♠
all pass			

With a slight shrug, West put the ♡K on the table. Tush felt the breath of doom even before the dummy came down. The full deal was:

Contract: 5♠ by South
Opening lead: ♡K

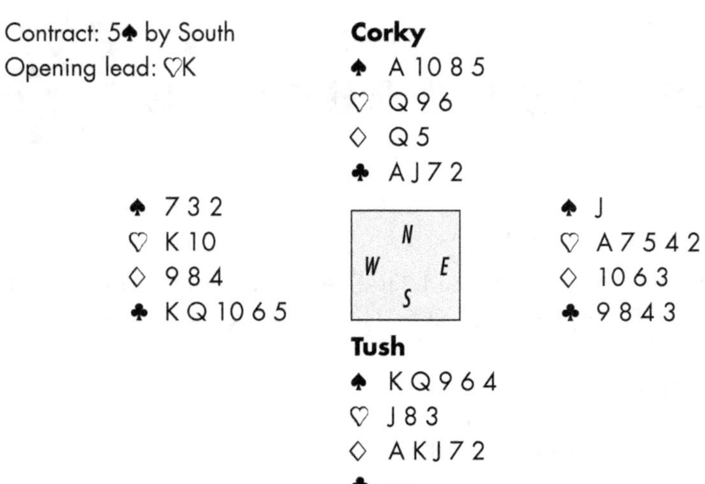

Corky
♠ A 10 8 5
♡ Q 9 6
◇ Q 5
♣ A J 7 2

♠ 7 3 2   ♠ J
♡ K 10   ♡ A 7 5 4 2
◇ 9 8 4   ◇ 10 6 3
♣ K Q 10 6 5   ♣ 9 8 4 3

Tush
♠ K Q 9 6 4
♡ J 8 3
◇ A K J 7 2
♣ —

The defense swiftly took the first three tricks with the two top hearts and a ruff; –50. Par was of course +420 for 4♠ making, so North-South were -10 IMPs.

"Nice lead," said Tush to West.

"On that auction, if I didn't lead a heart, you should probably play me for a void," he replied, a bit ungraciously.

"I thought about bidding six spades straightaway," said Tush, undaunted. "Seven might have worked even better. It would be nice if there were some way one could bid hands like this intelligently without giving away the lead."

Corky and the two opponents glanced at one another: who would take this bait?

It was Corky. "You've come to the right place, Robert. Stick around, you may get to see how it's done."

TUSH'S OPPONENT MISSES A PLAY

On the next deal, Tush held

♠ 10 7 5 2   ♡ A 9 6 5 4 2   ◊ 8 6   ♣ 4

as Corky opened second in hand with 1♣. When East overcalled with
1♠, Tush found himself wishing he had been playing negative free bids;
he really wanted to bid those hearts. But, even then, he only had 4
HCP. What was he stewing about, anyway? He was playing Yellow Card,
and he had to pass.

West advanced to 2◊, partner passed, and East cuebid 3♣.

Now Tush could not stop himself from stepping in with 3♡. He
was limited by his failure to bid or double the first time, right? That
this would be small consolation for a vulnerable disaster did not enter
his mind.

But Tush got away with it: West ended the auction with 3NT.

West	North	East	South
pass	1♣	1♠	pass
2◊	pass	3♣	3♡
3NT	all pass		

Corky's lead was the ♡8.

Contract: 3NT by West
Opening lead: ♡8

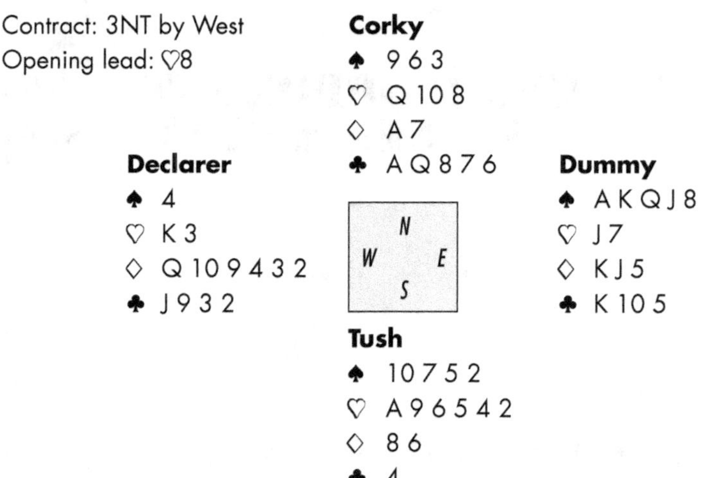

The first trick consisted of the ♡8, ♡7, ♡6 and ♡K. Trying unsuccessfully to look optimistic, West played out his spades, Tush throwing a diamond and Corky a couple of clubs. Finally declarer had to play diamonds; Corky lost no time in rising with the ace and playing queen and another heart to Tush. Five heart tricks and the two minor- suit aces made up the final seven tricks, and a tasty +300 to Tush and Corky — +9 IMPs, against the par of +110 East-West.

"I make it easily on a small club lead," West grumbled.

"You make it easily on the actual lead," said East, "if you play the jack of hearts from dummy at Trick 1."

Tush, Corky and West looked at one another. Huh!?

"Blocks the suit," East explained. Tush was stunned. Who could imagine that it made a difference which card was played from the board? Yet, indisputably, if declarer had played the jack, he and Corky would have been stymied.

"But that would be a double-dummy play!" West whined.

"Oh really?" countered East. "Your only chance for the contract, and you call that double-dummy? Jiminy Cricket! If you're going to bid like that, you have to play for the cards to be right."

Tush could not remember the last time he had heard anyone say "Jiminy Cricket." Poor West.

East-West left the table, both looking unhappy. "Whew," said Tush. "I'm glad we got back that bad board from them, even though we didn't exactly earn it."

"We learned something, too," said Corky. "Next time I get dealt queen-ten-eight in your suit, I'm going to lead a higher card!"

TUSH GETS HIS FIRST TASTE OF CRYPTO

Next to arrive at Tush's table were a young, friendly couple, who introduced themselves as Dan and Daniella. Brother and sister? They didn't say, but they did look somewhat alike to Tush. Pleasantries were exchanged and hands picked up.

Corky passed as dealer, and Dan, on Tush's right, opened 1♣. With

♠5　♡K 8 7 4　◇J 7 5 3　♣Q 9 5 2

Tush naturally passed. Daniella's 3NT response was alerted on Tush's display as:

```
FORCING RAISE WITH 2 OF THE TOP 3 TRUMPS
```

and opener's 4◇ rebid as:

```
ASKING FOR CONTROL
```

Daniella's 4♠ bid ended the auction. The bidding had been:

West	North	East	South
Daniella	Corky	Dan	Tush
	pass	1♠	pass
3NT	pass	4◇	pass
4♠	all pass		

"I presume 4♠ denies a diamond control?" said Tush to Dan, fingering the ◇3.

"It denies a control in the asked suit," replied Dan.

"The asked suit being diamonds, right?"

"Well, diamonds if I hold the spade ace, clubs if I hold the spade king, and hearts if I hold the spade queen."

"What if you don't hold any top trump?"

"Then I bid something else. Four spades, probably, unless I'm looking for a slam missing a top trump."

"Okay, I don't really get what all this top trump stuff is all about. Can't you or your partner just tell me which suit your four diamond bid asked about, in this deal?"

"Robert, you're missing the point," said Corky. "They don't have to tell you which suit. That's information they have from looking at their own cards. Dan only has to tell you what Daniella's bid *could* mean, and vice-versa."

It took a minute for Tush to absorb this. Clearly, both opponents knew which suit the inquiry was in, because they both knew which top trump was alone in the East hand. Presumably, Dan could have asked in the other suits by bidding 4♣ or 4♡. But what was the point of all this nonsense?

Glancing down at his table display, Tush read:

YOUR LEAD AGAINST 4♠ BY EAST

Of course, that was the answer: *Tush had no idea what to lead.*

Stalling for time, Tush turned to Daniella. "What would you have responded with a forcing raise and only one top trump?"

"Two notrump would have shown one top trump and at least a limit raise," she said. "With a slammish hand and the other two trump tops opener can bid at the four-level using the same scheme, except of course that the lone top trump is now in responder's hand."

"How do you keep this asking-bid scheme in your head? Don't you have to memorize a whole system for each distribution of the trump tops?"

"Oh, it's easy," said Dan. "The rule is: 'Ace is honest, king lies over, queen lies under.' For example, if the lone top is the queen, and I want to ask about diamonds, I bid four clubs—in other words, I lie by bidding one under the intended suit. Of course, the trump suit is skipped in the rotation."

Turning again to Daniella: "And what if you don't have any trump tops?"

"Then I respond with a forcing one notrump. That works out well, it turns out. When I later jump raise, my partner is warned about trump quality. In practice, knowing about trump quality—"

"Listen," interrupted Dan darkly, "no matter how many questions you ask, you're never going to find out what suit the asking bid was for."

"All right, all right. Give me a second here."

Tush stared at his hand. Would've been nice to have an ace–king to lead from. Or if his partner had doubled something for a lead—but, come to think of it, she'd never had that opportunity. Damn.

Eventually Tush came out with a Solomonic trump lead, the full deal being:

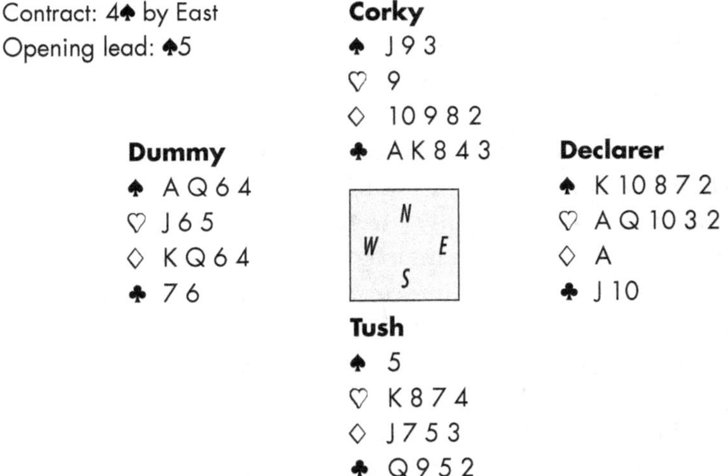

East quickly won Corky's trump jack with his king, unblocked the ◇A, drew the rest of the trumps ending on the board, and pitched his club losers on dummy's diamond tops.

The heart finesse lost, so that was −480 for Tush and Corky, against −420 par. Tush was thankful that only two IMPs had been at stake, but it bothered him that his opponents had been able to bid this hand intelligently without giving away the club lead. Was this even legal?

"Um, I don't mean to be critical," Tush lied, turning to his right-hand opponent, "but isn't this against the spirit of full disclosure in bridge? Am I not entitled to understand your auction?"

"Only what the bids mean, not what cards we hold. And you know exactly what my four diamonds meant: either I had the spade ace and was asking about diamonds, or the spade king and was..."

"Okay, I've seen either-or bids before, but once you both know which meaning is the right one, shouldn't I be told?"

Daniella joined the discussion. "Suppose you and your partner are on your way to a slam, and you bid four notrump, and your partner shows an ace, and you bid five notrump, showing the rest of the aces."

"And?"

"Well, you now know which ace your partner has, right?"

"Sure."

"If I, your opponent, ask you which ace she holds, do you tell me?"

"Of course not, but that's not the same thing, nothing hangs on which ace she holds."

"That's because you didn't hang anything on it. On that auction you and your partner developed two bits worth of cryptographic 'key' that you could theoretically use to hide information."

Tush felt out of his depth. "Two bits? You mean, twenty-five cents? And what's this about the key to a crypt?"

"No, no, 'bits' like in computers: zeros and ones. Cryptology is the science of secret codes. If you want to communicate with your partner secretly, you need some shared information that the opponents don't have. In this case, you and your partner know which of the four possible aces she has. You could think of that as two bits of information, for example, one bit to say whether the ace is red or black, another to say whether it's in a major suit or a minor."

"Are you saying, if you want to *tell* a secret, you have to *have* a secret?"

"Exactly! In this case, the secret Dan and I share is which top trump Dan has. We use this to communicate the identity of the suit of his asking bid, by tying it to the shared secret."

"Okay, I think I follow you, but, regardless, shouldn't all this have been explained to me and my partner in advance?"

"Would that change anything? What's your defense?"

Tush had no answer.

"Don't fret," said Dan mildly. "Since the early days of contract bridge, everyone thought that the rule forbidding prior private understandings prevented communication in secret. That's had rather a stultifying effect on bidding theory for almost a century. Why work to develop a fancy slam-bidding system, if it's going to tell the opponents what to lead? But, as you can see, sometimes you can eat your cake and have it too."

After Dan and Daniella excused themselves for refreshment, Corky caught Tush's attention with a whisper.

"Sorry about all that politicking," she said. "I'm told this club was founded by a bunch of former cryptanalysts. P-G himself is supposed to have helped break the Ho Chi Minh code during Vietnam. They can be a bit fanatical with their applications of cryptography to bridge."

"Honestly, I can't believe this kind of thing comes up often enough to make it worth while," Tush groused.

Corky laughed. "Just wait!"

TUSH USES CRYPTO HIMSELF

Second-in-hand, Tush picked up

♠ 1 0 9 5   ♡ Q J 8 5 4   ◇ K 3   ♣ J 7 2

and passed quickly when Dan opened 1♡ at his right. Daniella responded 1NT, Corky passed, and Dan now leapt to 3♡.

Tush knew better than to double—they could well be going on to 3NT or even 4♡. But no, Daniella now passed. And Corky doubled! Three passes followed.

West	North	East	South
Daniella	Corky	Dan	Tush
		1♡	pass
1NT	pass	3♡	pass
pass	dbl	all pass	

Tush led the ♠10, and Daniella put her hand down with a whispered "Good luck" to her partner.

Dummy
- ♠ J 6 3
- ♡ 3
- ◇ Q 9 7 5 2
- ♣ K 8 4 3

Tush
- ♠ 10 9 5
- ♡ Q J 8 5 4
- ◇ K 3
- ♣ J 7 2

Declarer, Dan, pursed his lips and turned to Tush. "How do you take your partner's double?"

"We, er, haven't discussed this auction."

"But you probably have some idea, right?"

Tush thought about this carefully. "Well, I guess if I were in her position, I'd hope that partner could tell by his trump length whether it was for penalty or takeout."

"So, you know what your partner's double means, but you're refusing to tell me?"

"Well, I…" Tush suddenly realized that Dan was grinning. So were Corky and Daniella, for that matter.

"It seems," Corky remarked, "that you and I were using cryptologic methods, without even having discussed it. Good thing we're at this club. In some venues, two-way doubles would theoretically be illegal."

It did indeed seem, thought Tush, that this method of nailing the opponents left them in the dark as to which defender had the trump length—information that might be useful in the play. Speaking of which, declarer had won Tush's spade lead with the queen, cashed the aces of diamonds and spades, and exited with a spade to Tush's nine, dummy's jack and Corky's king. Corky led deuce of trumps.

Declarer stared at this card, then at Corky, then at Tush. Who had the trumps? Finally, he played the nine; jack, three.

Now the ball was in Tush's court. Clubs looked iffy, but letting declarer ruff the ◇K with a small trump and work some trump endplay looked worse. So Tush tried a club, which rode to Corky's nine and declarer's queen. The layout in fact was:

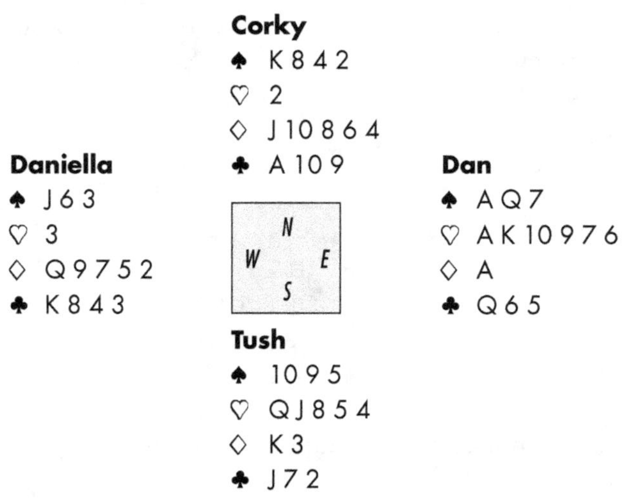

Not looking happy, Dan played another club to the jack, king and Corky's ace. Corky cashed the ♣10 and played the thirteenth spade, ruffed by declarer's six and Tush's eight. Tush still had the ♢K to exit with, and took the last trick with the trump queen.

That was +500 to Tush and Corky, and twelve IMPs; par was −120 North-South for 2NT by East or West.

Dan shook his head. "I can hold it to down one if I know South has the trumps. I go up when they lead a trump through; then he can't escape a trump endplay. Damn! At least we stopped short of game. I almost jump shifted. Shoot, some people will open with two clubs."

"They defended well. I'm betting the field is in four hearts doubled, down two."

"Maybe. Anyway,"—to Tush and Corky—"good luck to you both."

As they left the table, Tush glanced appreciatively at Corky. That double was quite a call; he wasn't sure he'd even have thought of it.

TUSH SWINDLES HIS RIGHT-HAND OPPONENT

"Very unlucky trump break," said East to his partner as he sat down. "Don't worry, the whole club will be in game."

About to warn them not to discuss hands, Tush realized that they were talking about the deal he and Corky had just played—thus, no harm, no foul. Definitely one of the advantages of playing the boards in parallel.

East had a loud voice and an even louder sweater, one of those Australian things with all the colors of the rainbow. His partner, a more demurely dressed young woman, had the pose, but not the eye response, of an attentive listener.

Picking up

♠ K 8 4　♡ K Q J 10 2　♢ K 7　♣ 9 6 5

Tush opened 1♡ as dealer, was raised to 2♡ and, amazingly, allowed to play there.

West	North	East	South
			1♡
pass	2♡	all pass	

Contract: 2♡ by South
Opening lead: ♠5

Dummy
♠　10 7 3
♡　9 6 3
♢　J 10 5 3
♣　K Q J

Tush
♠　K 8 4
♡　K Q J 10 2
♢　K 7
♣　9 6 5

The ♣5 was led to the ♣A, and the ♠2 returned. The opponents' silence suggested that there was not likely to be any ruffing danger, so, surely, thought Tush, this was going to come down to guessing the diamonds. Was there anything else available?

Not really thinking it through, he won the ♠K (West following with the ♠6) and played a club. Dummy's ♣J won, drawing the ♣2 and ♣3, and a trump back to Tush's queen held as well. Trying to look like he wanted to lead trumps from the board again, Tush put another club on the table; this time West rose with the ace and played the ♠J, overtaken by his partner's queen.

East now descended into deep thought, and Tush could see that declarer's job was to not look self-satisfied. Having been dealt something like

$$\spadesuit A Q 9 2 \quad \heartsuit A x x \quad \diamondsuit ? ? x \quad \clubsuit x x x$$

and placing his partner with the trump jack, Loud Sweater must be thinking about a trump promotion. Finally he fell for it, placing the ♠9 on the table. Tush pitched his small diamond, ruffed on the board, and racked up his contract with professional demeanor.

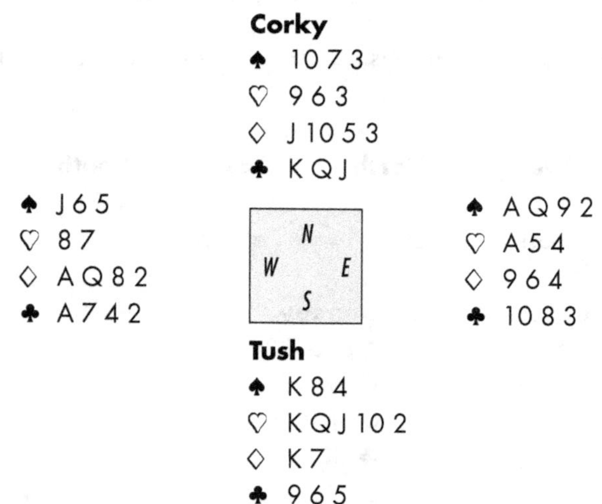

Corky
♠ 10 7 3
♡ 9 6 3
♢ J 10 5 3
♣ K Q J

West		East
♠ J 6 5		♠ A Q 9 2
♡ 8 7		♡ A 5 4
♢ A Q 8 2		♢ 9 6 4
♣ A 7 4 2		♣ 10 8 3

Tush
♠ K 8 4
♡ K Q J 10 2
♢ K 7
♣ 9 6 5

Plus 110 was worth 6 gratifying IMPs against the par of −110 for 2♠ by East-West.

"I wanted to tell you about my ace and queen of diamonds," said West to her partner, "but I didn't see how."

"Not your fault," said East quickly. "I was trying to promote your jack of hearts. Otherwise I would have led a diamond for you."

"But I didn't have the jack of hearts."

"Well, you might've had it. Just one of those things, I had to play the odds."

"Were the odds"—this from an innocent-looking Corky—"that declarer would have no diamond loser to throw on the thirteenth spade?"

I don't think Corky likes this guy, thought Tush to himself.

East's face began to take on some of the colors of his sweater. "He might have had king–queen doubleton of diamonds, for example, along with king–queen–ten fifth of trump."

"I almost did have that," said Tush magnanimously. He felt a certain empathy toward Loud Sweater—another guy trying to impress a girl. There, but for the grace of God…

TUSH FINDS A DELICATE DISCOVERY PLAY

On the next board West opened 1♡ as dealer, described by the table as

RICOCHET: 5+ HEARTS, 11-15 HCP

Tush remembered seeing Ricochet among his system options; apparently it was some kind of big club system. In any case, this call was doubled by Corky and raised to 2♡ by Loud Sweater.

Holding

♠5 4 3 2   ♡A 6 2   ◇K 8 7 2   ♣9 3

Tush typed in 2♠ without much thought—then it hit him. Did he really just make a free bid on a five-high suit? Did he want partner to raise that suit, or, even worse, lead it? Should he have made a responsive double instead? No—stick to your guns, Tush! Partner has doubled 1♡, and you have the master suit: you must bid it.

Tush was visibly nervous when his partner bid 4♠ over West's 4♡ call, but no one doubled. The auction had been:

West	North	East	South
1♡	dbl	2♡	2♠
4♡	4♠	all pass	

The ♡K was led and dummy came down.

Contract: 4♠ by South
Opening lead: ♡K

Dummy
♠ A K Q 6
♡ —
◇ A Q 6 5 3
♣ 10 7 6 4

Tush
♠ 5 4 3 2
♡ A 6 2
◇ K 8 7 2
♣ 9 3

"Thank you, partner," said Tush with feeling. What a great dummy! Even with void opposite ace, the fit was gorgeous. Tush counted eleven tricks: four trumps, five diamonds, the ♡A and a heart ruff, if the trumps and diamonds behaved. What an easy hand, too: no card combinations in any suit, just tops and bottoms.

Of course, a four-one trump split, especially four with East, was a lively possibility—East didn't seem to have given any thought to sacrificing. But there was a trick to spare, after all. Ruff the opening lead, draw three rounds of trump, then play diamonds; they can ruff when they like.

Oops, no they can't: if they ruff the fourth round, the last diamond winner would be marooned in dummy. Better to draw only two rounds of trump; then when the diamond is ruffed, dummy can be re-entered with a trump to finish the suit.

With his mouth open to call for a small trump from the board, Tush reconsidered. Was it safe to leave two trumps out? If East had a stiff diamond, he could ruff the second round of diamonds and put his partner in with a club to score a fatal encore diamond ruff.

Come to think of it, if East had, say,

♠ J 10 9 8　♡ x x x x　◇ x x x　♣ K x

he could ruff a diamond and then score a club ruff. Nothing Tush's microscopic trumps could do to stop that!

In fact, thought Tush, even a 2-2 diamond split wasn't safe. If East had two diamonds and three clubs, he could pitch a club on the third round of diamonds, then ruff the fourth diamond and set the contract with a club ruff. Yikes! Was he good enough to do that? Out of the corner of his eye, Tush could see Loud Sweater thinking hard, well motivated to get revenge for the previous deal. And Tush was certainly providing him with lots of time for analysis.

Tush concentrated. Maybe there's another way to play this. Suppose the heart ruff is saved for later, as a re-entry. Win the opening lead in hand, cash the three top trumps, then play diamonds. Sweet! Now they could ruff whenever they liked; Tush could get back to the board with his heart ruff to finish the diamonds.

Tush liked this line, but then another thought struck him: what if they never ruff? Then when he exits in clubs, they draw trumps and take the last four tricks! Ah, but wait: there was a counter to that. All Tush had to do was win the fourth round of diamonds in hand, then take his heart ruff before playing the last diamond.

Tush was conscious of three pairs of eyes waiting for him to play from dummy, but he had made himself declarer with a dubious trump holding and now was determined to play the hand right. Was there any flaw in this last plan? Yes, East might pitch hearts on diamonds and later overruff the heart, marooning the last diamond once again. Shoot!

Well, to do that he would need to have been dealt a singleton diamond, or two diamonds and only three hearts. Tush couldn't see any way to make the hand against good defense, if East had a stiff diamond. But if he indeed had two diamonds and three hearts, the old plan of drawing only two trumps was safe.

What was needed was a way to combine the two plans, and make the contract whenever it could be made. A way to do that was slowly taking shape in Tush's brain. At last, Tush called for a club from dummy and won the lead in hand with the $\heartsuit$A, then played a trump to the ace and then the king.

Wouldn't you know it, West showed out on the second round, throwing a heart. Tush was relieved to see this; at least he hadn't wasted all that time on a non-existent problem. He called for the $\diamondsuit$A. "No! Wait!" he blurted. "The three! I meant the three!"

Lowered eyebrows from all three other players accosted Tush, but with shrugs, East and West indicated that they would allow the three to be played from the board. Tush had realized, almost too late, that to put his plan in action a high diamond had to be led from the board on the third round of the suit—and this meant that Tush had to win the first round in hand with the king.

Next Tush led the ◊7 back to the ace, both opponents following. Had West proved to be the owner of a second singleton, the plan involving the late heart ruff would have been assured. Tush would have cashed another trump and played more diamonds, winning the fourth round in hand if no one ruffed, then taken his heart ruff before leading the fifth diamond.

With diamonds 2-2, Tush continued with the queen as planned. East's play to this trick was critical. If he ruffed, East-West could cash two clubs but would then have to let declarer draw the last trump and claim. If he pitched a club, Tush would follow with the ◊2, then lead to the ◊8 with the late heart ruff again planned.

In fact, East threw a heart; now Tush unblocked the ◊8, and continued with the ◊6 from the board. What could East do? Ruffing was hopeless; dummy was waiting with a good diamond and the ♠Q, poised to draw the last trump. North-South's remaining small trumps would be made separately.

So East threw another heart, but it did him no good; Tush played yet a fifth diamond, throwing a club from hand. Pursuing his only remaining hope (to stop declarer from making a fourth trump trick), East discarded once more. But Tush exited the board with a club and could not be prevented from scoring a club ruff in hand for his tenth trick.

The full deal lit up on the table.

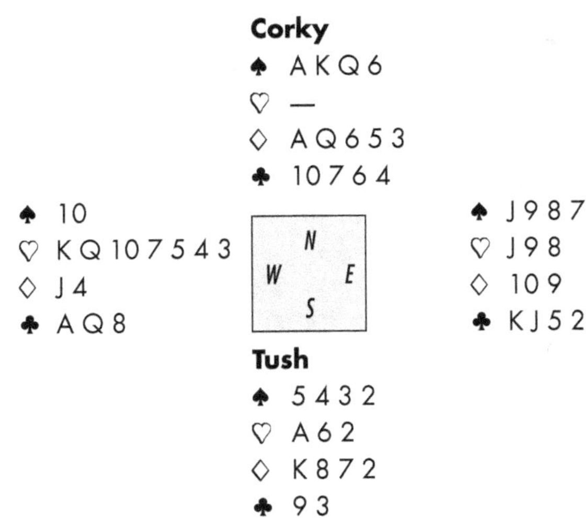

Par was +300 to N-S for defeating 5♥, doubled by two tricks. Three IMPs to Tush and Corky for their +420.

"Was that some kind of squeeze?" asked West. "Was that why you had to play the diamonds the way you did?"

Tush beamed. "It's true that my play depended on what your partner discarded," he explained. "But his problem is not that he has to discard; his problem is that he can't discard enough cards. Sort of an anti-squeeze, except that there's no hand he can hold that offers both defenses, so I guess it's technically a discov…"

The table was flashing "change of round" and the opponents were already moving, so Tush's monologue was cut mercifully short. But he did get his first-ever smile from Corky, and a couple of mouthed words which Tush took to be "Nice play."

Alas, the words didn't quite match her mouth movement. Tush got only about thirty seconds of enjoyment before realizing that what she had actually said was "Nice suit."

TUSH DEFENDS WELL, BUT...

A self-satisfied looking couple approached the table and introduced themselves as Dean and Glenda. They must have a good game going, thought Tush. Maybe I can put a crimp in it.

Corky opened 1♠ as dealer, and Tush responded 1NT holding

♠ J 3 ♡ Q 5 2 ◇ K 10 7 4 3 2 ♣ 10 3

Then Dean and Glenda took over.

West	North	East	South
Dean	Corky	Glenda	Tush
	1♠	pass	1NT
2♡	pass	4♡	all pass

The ♡6 was led and dummy came down.

Contract: 4♡ by West
Opening lead: ♡6

Dummy
♠ 8 7 4 2
♡ K 8 4 3
◇ Q 8
♣ K 8 5

Tush
♠ J 3
♡ Q 5 2
◇ K 10 7 4 3 2
♣ 10 3

Declarer—Dean—took a moment to study the hands, during which time Tush reflected that (a) he, Tush, was certainly not going to go up with the ♡Q, and (b) it was interesting that his partner chose to lead what must surely be her only trump. Finally declarer called for the ♡8, which held the trick, then asked for the ◇8.

Tush had detached the $\Diamond$7 from his hand, and it was almost on the table, before he thought: better to balk than to blunder. What was declarer up to? Should Tush be rising with the king to return a trump, trying to prevent two diamond ruffs on the board? No, wait, that was ridiculous: if declarer had jack-fourth of diamonds, that would leave partner with the stiff ace, and second-hand-high would come spectacularly a cropper.

But, thought Tush, partner can't have two red singletons, or she'd have found some bid over 2$\heartsuit$. More likely she has the ace and some small diamonds, in which case perhaps it might be a good idea to go up with the king and lead a spade through, maybe take partner off of an endplay or a squeeze. Oops, wait: could declarer have $\Diamond$Ax and be hoping to throw partner in at the next trick? Nah, he'd probably draw trumps first, and anyway Corky must have something in diamonds that she didn't want to lead from.

It occurred to Tush that perhaps he should have put up the $\heartsuit$Q at Trick 1 after all, then he wouldn't have this problem—at least, not until after he'd seen a signal from partner.

Well, it was too late to play low nonchalantly, that was for sure. Tush replaced the $\Diamond$7 with the $\Diamond$K and breathed a mental sigh when it held the trick, declarer following with the jack. Tush's $\spadesuit$J drew the king and ace; Corky continued with the $\spadesuit$Q and then the $\Diamond$A, ruffed by declarer.

Well, thought Tush, that turned out fine; if partner has something good in clubs, we've got this beat. Declarer, looking a bit peeved, cashed the $\heartsuit$K and $\heartsuit$A, paused briefly, then shrugged his shoulders and pulled the $\clubsuit$J out of his hand. Seconds later, Corky was typing –620.

The full deal:

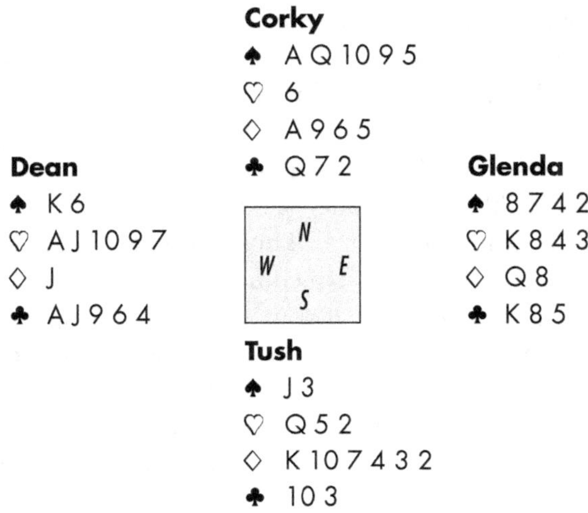

"Nicely defended," said Dean with a nod toward Tush. "If you don't hop up with the king of diamonds, I can later throw your partner in with the third round of clubs and hold my spade losers to one. Bad luck for you in clubs; if she has the ten, your defense beats the hand."

Tush savored the compliment. "Well, I think we've achieved par, anyway. There's no way to beat four hearts."

"Or four spades," said Corky. "We lose thirteen IMPs."

Tush's eyes widened. "What!? Are you serious?"

Sure enough, a glance at the table confirmed that North-South had ten unstoppable tricks in spades; par was +200 North-South, for 5♡ or 5♣ by East-West doubled and down one. "This is outrageous," Tush wailed. "Look at just our two hands: four spades *stinks!*"

Dean laughed. "It does, but the five-diamond sacrifice is reasonable, down only one."

"Oh, really?" Tush blurted, pride at his expert defense a distant memory. "And how are we supposed to find that fit?"

"You could respond two diamonds to the opening bid. Glenda or I would have."

Tush was livid. "Give me a break—I'm an ace and a half short for a two-over-one, even by Goren standards."

"Take it easy," Corky soothed. "He's not saying you should have bid it. In Ricochet, two-over-one is not forcing."

"You're kidding me, right? I mean, surely that's not playable?"

"Of course, it helps that opener is limited in a big club system, and with a strong hand responder has a one notrump response available."

Tush was aware that he had lost his composure, but getting it back was going to be difficult under these circumstances. "Are you all aware that the rest of the world has been *raising* the requirements for a two-over-one?"

"Not in competition," Corky replied. "Suppose your right-hand opponent had doubled one spade. These days, lots of people would bid two diamonds with your hand. Those who play negative free bids might bid two diamonds after a two club overcall, as well."

"Plus," interjected Glenda, "if your partner's one spade had itself been an overcall, your two diamond bid would be non-forcing there, as well, no? When you've got a six-card suit and a chance to bid it at the two-level, shouldn't your system allow you to do that?"

"Those are all competitive situations," Tush argued. "You need to have some foundation for constructive bidding when it's your hand."

"Part of the theory of Ricochet," Corky explained patiently, "is that nowadays you won't be far wrong if you assume every low-level auction is competitive. Then, you can do what Ricochet does, which is to keep it simple by having the same agreements with or without interference."

"Glenda and I used to play a sort of Eastern Scientific," said Dean. "But there was too much to memorize. We began running a beginners' class, and we had so much fun teaching them Richochet, we decided to try it ourselves. It ain't perfect, that's for sure, but it has a consistent logic to it."

"Okay, okay, I get the point," said Tush. But, to himself, he thought: Man, there are some weird ideas running around this club. Sooner or later, they were due to bring him some unearned IMPs.

TUSH FINDS A MASTER BID

On the next board, both sides vulnerable, Tush picked up a modest three-suiter, second to speak:

$$\spadesuit\,— \quad \heartsuit\,10\,7\,5\,2 \quad \diamondsuit\,A\,K\,9\,4 \quad \clubsuit\,9\,8\,5\,3\,2$$

Glenda passed, as did Tush; Dean opened 1♣, described in front of Tush as RICOCHET: ARTIFICIAL AND FORCING, 16+ HCP. Corky overcalled 2♡ and (after an enforced pause) Glenda doubled to show general values and 9+ HCP. The auction had been:

West	North	East	South
Dean	Corky	Glenda	Tush
		pass	pass
1♣	2♡	dbl	?

What now? West obviously had a big spade hand, and raising Corky's hearts to four was too wimpy a bid to even consider. Some five-level bid was surely indicated, and the obvious choice was between a straightforward 5♡ and a lead-directing 5♢. The latter seemed safe enough, but it would be rather a shame to go to all that trouble to prevent East-West from cuebidding, then tell them exactly where their hole was. For example, if Dean were to bid 5♠ over Tush's 5♢, Glenda would know not to raise without a diamond control.

Encryption would be handy here, Tush grudgingly admitted to himself. Some way to tell Corky to lead a diamond, without telling the opponents. Maybe if he had the ♡A or ♡K.... no, what's the point in even thinking about that? He and Corky would need to have had an agreement already in place.

But in the meantime another idea crept into Tush's mind, and the outcome was a master bid of five *clubs*. When he pushed the buttons, instead of registering his call, the display came back with a question for Tush:

What is this, thought Tush: a survey? In the middle of an auction? Then it came to him: the computer was offering Tush a chance to commit to an action, so that he could take it even over a slow pass or slow double by partner. Interesting idea, but no thanks on this hand. Tush answered 'no' and his 5♣ call appeared.

Dean thought for a bit, then entered 6♠ on his touchpad. Corky took, perforce, the required ten seconds to pass, while Tush sweated. After East's pass, Tush doubled, ending the auction.

West	North	East	South
Dean	Corky	Glenda	Tush
		pass	pass
1♣	2♡	dbl	5♣
6♠	pass	pass	dbl
all pass			

Trying to look casual, Tush prayed. He'd bid clubs, then asked for an unusual lead. So, Corky would have to lead a diamond, right? Come on, come on…

A moment of elation came over Tush as Corky's ◇8 hit the table, quickly extinguished as the board came down with diamond after diamond.

Contract: 6♠ by West
Opening lead: ◇8

Dummy
♠ Q 8 3
♡ J 6
◇ Q J 6 5 3 2
♣ K 7

Tush
♠ —
♡ 10 7 5 2
◇ A K 9 4
♣ 9 8 5 3 2

   Bridge at the Enigma Club

A small diamond was called for from the table. Well, thought Tush, either that eight was stiff or it wasn't, so, with nothing in mind but general trickiness, Tush played his ace—declarer dropping the ten—and led the four back.

Dean knitted his very substantial brows, glaring first at Tush and then at Corky. Clearly, he was out of diamonds, but worried about an overruff. Tush realized now that his concealment of the diamond king had been a transparent falsecard, but the fortuitous result was that declarer thought Tush was trying to make him believe it was safe to ruff low. Maybe Dean would think Tush was attempting to protect some trump holding. Despite not knowing how to do it, Tush tried to look like someone who was trying to look innocent.

Finally declarer ruffed with the ♠K and continued with the ♠10 out of hand. When Corky followed low without apparent thought, he again tanked, finally putting up the board's queen.

When Tush showed out, Dean threw down his cards with a shocking expletive. The full deal had been:

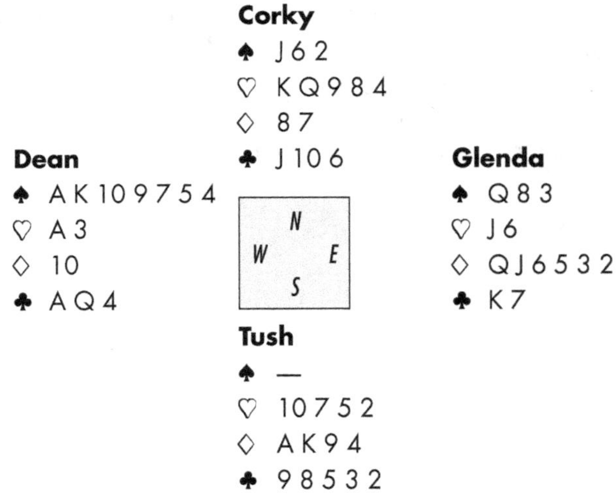

Tush could hardly believe his luck—his bidding ploy had not merely beaten a vulnerable slam, it had beaten a *makeable* vulnerable slam. But let's not forget to give some credit to partner. "Thank—"

"You blockhead!" screamed the previously well-modulated Glenda to her partner, her eyes on the table display. Then, switching to a strained whisper, "You think he has long diamonds, long spades, and enough hearts to go to the five-level?"

"Hey, give me a break, okay? Maybe he was bidding clubs on a void, to get a lead."

"Right, and how many clubs does that leave in the heart hand?"

"Um, a lot, okay, but, come on, something's fishy about this whole deal, and I didn't want to go down with the trumps splitting."

An imposing man with crew-cut white hair materialized at the table side. "Can we keep it down a bit here? Remember, others are playing the same deal."

Dean looked up, hands spread. "Sorry, P-G. Got carried away. Won't happen again."

"Better not," said Glenda under her breath.

Corky, in the meantime, was entering the result: +100 N-S meant 17 IMPs for the good guys (par was -1400 for 7♡ doubled, by N-S). "That was quite an imaginative call, five clubs," she said to Tush. "I thought about putting you in seven."

"Our vulnerability made it less likely, I figured, that you would sacrifice," said Tush. And the Lord above helped too, he thought. He and Corky had a great game going and she was proving to be a perfect 'straight man' for Tush's flights of fancy. Not bad to look at, either, especially now that her mood had improved. He could easily imagine a permanent arrangement, and not just for bridge. One of them would need to move, of course, but—

"Good luck," said Dean as he and Glenda packed up to change tables. But his tone suggested that he thought Tush and Corky had already had more than their share.

TUSH DERAILS ANOTHER SLAM

Two women, both in their mid-forties and expensively dressed, had quietly replaced Dean and Glenda in the East-West chairs. They looked grim—things must not be going well. At least they didn't seem to be angry at each other. Tush's table display said they were playing Ricochet, and indeed they proceeded to use the system to get to slam.

West	North	East	South
			pass
1♣	pass	2♣	pass
2♠	pass	3♠	pass
4◇	pass	4♡	pass
4NT	pass	5♣	pass
5◇	pass	5♡	pass
6♠	all pass		

The opening bid had been a big club (16+ HCP), the 2♣ response natural and positive. The 4♡ bid was explained as "last train," tending to show a card in opener's second suit (diamonds); subsequently responder had shown one key card plus the queen of trumps.

Corky led the ♡4.

Contract: 6♠ by West
Opening lead: ♡4

Dummy
♠ Q 9 4
♡ J 8 3
◇ K 4
♣ A 9 7 6 3

Tush
♠ K J 5 3
♡ Q 10 9 6
◇ J 9 5
♣ J 8

Declarer played the ♡8 from the board and won Tush's nine with the ace, then took a moment to think.

Tush was not optimistic; the ♡A smelled like a singleton, diamonds were breaking for declarer, and even if Corky had the ten of trumps, Tush's trump holding could be picked up with the loss of only one trick.

In fact, it was declarer who led the ♠10 to Trick 2, Corky following with the ♠2. The queen was played from dummy and Tush, on the theory that something had to be done to deflect declarer, ducked smoothly. It was an example of what Tush thought of as the 'principle of derailment'—when declarer is headed for a make, try to get the train to jump the track.

Declarer immediately played a spade back to her ace, and had another card ready to lead from hand when the red flash of Corky's heart discard caught her eye.

"Um, spades were led," she said to Corky, failing to comprehend that she had been hornswoggled by Tush.

Corky pretended to look through her cards, while East gave her partner an icy look and Tush sat innocently. Eventually declarer played on diamonds and conceded two tricks to Tush's top trumps.

The full deal lit up on the table.

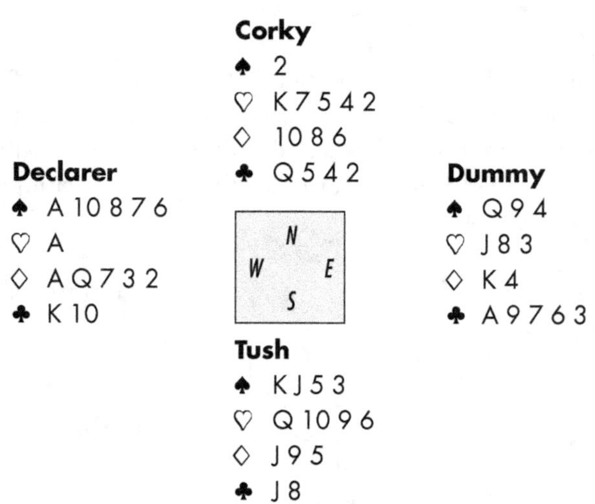

West spread her hands plaintively. "Obviously, if I know that diamonds are going to break, I take the safety play in trumps."

East sighed and shook her head, wisely deciding not to pursue the matter.

Par was −980 to North-South for 6♠ by East-West, but the 14 IMPs were not half as satisfying to Tush as the effect on his opponents—and, even more, the appreciative raised eyebrow and canted nod from his partner. It took all Tush's willpower to stop himself from pumping a triumphant, Brett-Favre-like fist in the air, and crying "Yesssss!!"

Instead, Tush mused: Damn, IMPs is fun. After this, can I ever go back to matchpoints?

TUSH FINDS A LEAD

Fourth to speak, Tush found himself looking at a junky nine-pointer:

♠ Q 10 9 2   ♡ 7 6   ◇ K 3 2   ♣ K J 9 2

West and North passed and it was East's turn to open with a big club, 16+ HCP. With Tush and Corky passing throughout, West responded with 1◇, negative—fewer than 9 HCP. East's 1♡ rebid was described by the table display as

WAITING FOR DESCRIPTION

West now bid 2♡—the table had no comment—and East raised to 7♡! The auction had been:

West	North	East	South
pass	pass	1♣	pass
1◇	pass	1♡	pass
2♡	pass	7♡	all pass

In view of the fact that he was about to make a possibly critical opening lead against a grand, Tush decided to get all the information he could. "Um, I haven't had much experience with—what do you call it? Ricochet? Can I get some general explanation before I lead?"

"By all means," said East. "Ricochet uses natural relays and always has a neutral response available. Partner's one diamond reply to my big club is a typical Ricochet neutral; it keeps the bidding open, but says 'I have nothing to describe at the moment.' Her other choices are natural and game forcing, so she either had no decent suit to show, or not enough points to show it. She'd need nine points, normally, or three honor tricks."

West picked up the thread. "My partner's one heart relay says nothing about her hand except that, by implication, it must be very strong. It's forcing and asks me to describe my hand naturally."

"My partner could now have bid one spade, again neutral, with a really bad hand," said East. "After that, one notrump by me would show nineteen to twenty-one high-card points, balanced; I'd have had to bid two clubs to continue relaying, with a mountain. Of course, she didn't bid one spade, she bid two hearts, which is natural, usually five decent hearts."

"Seven hearts was presumably to play," said West, unnecessarily.

Tush stared at his cards. What, indeed, could East have to jump to seven? Obviously a huge two-suiter. And she'd need at least ace-king at the top of her second suit for her bid to make any sense, so that suit must be spades.

If so, Tush's good spades looked encouraging for the defense. Declarer (East, on account of that early 1♡ call) would have to ruff out that suit in dummy, and might need entries to her own hand to do it. A trump lead? Heavens, no, that might pickle Corky's holding and prevent her from overruffing a spade. What about the minors? Declarer ought to have the ace in one and a maybe a void in the other. Driving out that ace had to be Tush's objective.

In fact, if he's going to do that, thought Tush, he should surely lead the king. Yes! A Deschapelles coup on opening lead! No, wait, wasn't that the one where you sacrifice an honor to get an entry to partner? What do you call the one where the gambit destroys an opponent's entry? Oh yes, a Merrimac coup! Against the big hand, no less! Tush's eyes lit up. This would impress Corky, for sure. Hell, it might make the newspapers!

Now, which minor? There seemed to be no clue. On second thought, since Tush had more clubs than diamonds, if declarer had a void it was more likely to be in clubs. It was a thin argument, but what else did he have? With a silent prayer, Tush detached the ◇K from his collection.

Contract: 7♡ by East
Opening lead: ◇K

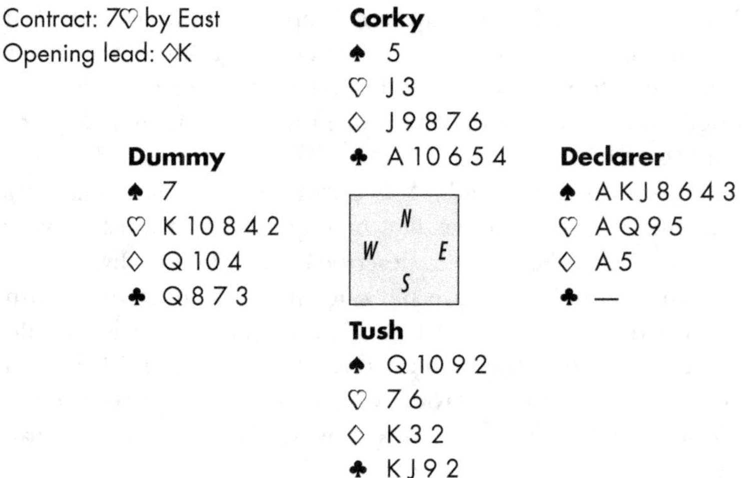

Corky
♠ 5
♡ J 3
◇ J 9 8 7 6
♣ A 10 6 5 4

Dummy
♠ 7
♡ K 10 8 4 2
◇ Q 10 4
♣ Q 8 7 3

Declarer
♠ A K J 8 6 4 3
♡ A Q 9 5
◇ A 5
♣ —

Tush
♠ Q 10 9 2
♡ 7 6
◇ K 3 2
♣ K J 9 2

Tush thought he saw Corky's eyes narrow slightly when his lead was captured by declarer's ace, but her composure was commendable. Declarer cashed the trump ace and paused to mull things over, chin in hand. Finally she played her ♠A and continued with a small one, looking a bit disappointed when Tush followed. Another hesitation.

Declarer stared at Corky. So did Tush. Corky looked bored.

Shrugging, declarer ruffed with the ♡8. No longer bored, Corky pounced on the trick with her ♡J. West looked upward and stretched her arms in supplication. "I don't believe it!" she cried, straining to look at Corky's remaining cards. "You can't just draw trump and claim, like everyone else in the room?"

"I'm not clairvoyant, you know," said East. "With that opening lead, I can make the hand even when neither major breaks, if there's no overruff. I went with the odds."

Up until then Tush had been engaged in working out how many IMPs he and Corky were raking in for defeating a makeable, non-vulnerable grand (17). But the mention of the opening lead made him sit up. What did his lead have to do with it? He stared at the table display, trying to see it through East's eyes. Declarer's line was a good one, needing only to avoid an overruff; she'd make the hand anytime Tush had fewer than four spades—assuming no one was void in a major—or if he had the ♡J.

But if Tush had led a *small* diamond, declarer would no doubt have misguessed, putting in the ♢10 from dummy. Then, she'd have had only six trump tricks, a diamond and five spades coming in if neither major broke. She'd have had nothing to lose by playing a second trump, and the slam would have rolled home when they broke 2-2.

In fact, *any* opening lead other than the ♢K would have led to a quick claim. A club would be ruffed in hand, ace–queen of trumps cashed, then ♠A and a small one ruffed with the ♡8 on the board. If spades didn't break, then, assuming no overruff, declarer would simply ruff another club in hand, ruff a second spade, draw the remaining trump (if any) with dummy's king, and claim with her ♢A and good spades in hand.

A trump lead would have forked poor Corky. If she covered the board's eight declarer would draw the second round from the board and ruff a club before turning to spades, this time not even worrying about an overruff. If she didn't cover, declarer would let the eight hold, ruff a club to hand, and continue as in the club lead case.

Of course, a spade lead into the ace–king–jack would have made it easy, so Tush had found the only lead to beat the contract. Was it a Merrimac coup? Well, sort of... Curious, though, that the gambit part—setting up an extra trick for the opponents—was necessary, not merely a cheap price for removing an entry.

After studying the table display, West was also beginning to see things through declarer's eyes. "Okay," she pouted to her partner, "maybe your line has some merit, but shoot, if you're going to bid like that, you need a little clairvoyance. Or better luck."

Not looking forward to a discussion of luck, Tush sought a deft change of topic. "Can I ask you a question," he said, turning to East, "about your partner's two heart call? Did it guarantee the king?"

"No," said East, "but suppose she has jack-ten fifth or sixth. Where do I want to play?"

Tush saw the point. On a diamond lead, with the trump king offside, East-West might not even be able to make six. May as well be in seven, playing for all the marbles.

"Hmmpf. Good bid. Sorry about the result."

"You're a liar, but thanks," said East as she gathered up her stuff.

X X X

With the opponents gone, Tush saw Corky looking at him suspiciously. "That's the third slam in a row you've beaten. Either you are one lucky S.O.B.," she offered, "or…"

Tush tried to smile mysteriously. "One way or the other," he said, "I have a feeling we're halfway to a win."

"Ah, about that. I should have told you earlier, this is a two-session event. I hope you have no plans for the evening? The good news is, you get a free dinner."

TUSH FINDS A FOOLPROOF LINE

The next round brought two bespectacled gentlemen to the table, one in mid-monologue and the other in deep concentration. To Tush they both looked like professors from Central Casting. West sported a white beard, East a gray mustache. "On the other hand," said West, "if you use transfers by advancer, you can have it both ways."

East nodded, but it was difficult to be certain whether he was responding to his partner, or to some internal thought.

Corky opened 1◇ as dealer, and Tush found himself holding nearly half the deck in his hands:

♠K 8 7 2   ♡A 4   ◇Q 6 4   ♣A K Q J

Even more surprising, Corky jumped to 4♣ over Tush's 1♠ response.

Tush didn't think splinters were on the Yellow Card, but what else could that call be? Obviously not strong clubs; must be a singleton with strong spade support. So he and Corky were facing serious wastage in clubs. Nonetheless it sounded like they might be able to take a lot of tricks on sheer power. Tush checked first for aces and kings, and when they all proved to be present and accounted for, he bid the grand in notrump so as to circumvent a possible spade loser.

West	North	East	South
Beard	Corky	Mustache	Tush
	1◇	pass	1♠
pass	4♣	pass	4NT
pass	5♡	pass	5NT
pass	6♡	pass	7NT
all pass			

The ♣10 was led and Corky put down her hand.

Contract: 7NT by South
Opening lead: ♣10

Dummy

♠ A Q 10 9
♡ K J 8 2
♢ A K 10 9
♣ 6

Tush

♠ K 8 7 2
♡ A 4
♢ Q 6 4
♣ A K Q J

Wow, thought Tush looking at the dummy: that was a splinter and a half! There were twelve tricks on top and formidable resources for a thirteenth. This looked like one of those cases where, if you play the spades intelligently, then even when the wrong opponent holds ♠Jxxx, a squeeze will come to the rescue.

But Tush couldn't quite see how he could guarantee the contract, no matter which way he played the spades. Well, the other thing he could do was to stave off playing the suit as long as possible. Hopefully, by the time he got to it, he'd either have his thirteenth trick bagged already, or he'd have enough of a count to rule out jack-fourth of spades by one opponent or the other.

Not seeing anything better, Tush won the opening lead and finished the clubs, somewhat reluctantly pitching three hearts from the board. On the last club, East threw a heart as well.

Next Tush led a heart to dummy's now bare king. It looked right to play diamonds ending in hand, so he could be there to cash the ♡A before facing the spade problem. Accordingly, Tush cashed the ♢A and ♢K and continued small to his queen, but no jack appeared. West threw his last club on the third round.

So, thought Tush, East has the ♢J. What else have I learned? Nothing. May as well cash the ♡A. West followed suit and Tush parted with the ♢10 from the board, reducing both his hand and the dummy's to all spades. East threw his now-worthless ♢J.

Shoot, thought Tush. No squeeze, no... wait a minute. Clubs had been 5-3, diamonds 2-4, hearts 5-2, so he had a complete count! Spades must be 1-4. Not completely trusting himself, Tush played to the ♠A and ♠Q, and, sure enough, West showed out. Tush finessed through East and had his thirteenth trick. Whew!

The full deal had been:

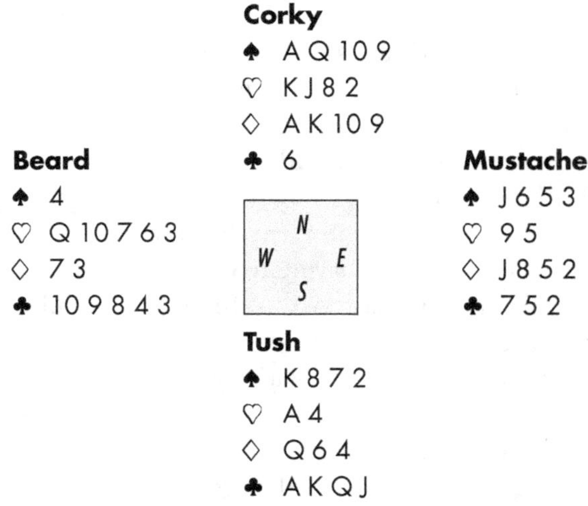

"I don't know what I'd have done if you hadn't shown out on the ace of hearts," Tush admitted to East.

"Nonsense," said East. "If I still have the jack of diamonds at the point when you're down to four spades in each hand, you know I can't have jack-fourth of spades, and you're home.

"Yes, your line is a hundred percent," West contributed. "By the time you get to the spades, if you haven't dropped the jack of diamonds, you either know where it is, or you have a count on the whole deal. It's a guaranteed discovery play."

"Nice going, partner," said Corky with a twinkling eye.

Tush shook his head. "I was sure there was a squeeze, but I couldn't see how to do it, and gave up."

East caressed his mustache thoughtfully. "Oh, but you did indeed squeeze me," he said. "On the fourth club, I had to throw a heart to avoid giving you your thirteenth trick outright. But that was costly too; it meant that I later had to show out on the second round of hearts, giving you the count."

"Great example of a non-material squeeze, à la Géza Ottlik," said Beard gleefully. "Even better, a squeeze for the count, instead of without the count!"

Tush must have looked dubious. "What, you don't agree?" asked Mustache.

"Seems like you're stretching the definition of 'squeeze' a bit far on this one," said Tush.

"Ah, but you can define the notion of 'squeeze' very precisely. Imagine a variation on the rules of play, where you may occasionally be given a 'discard waiver' and not have to play a card to some trick (to which you could not follow suit). Of course, play still ceases after thirteen tricks.

"Now, if at some point you must discard and every choice damages your side relative to having a discard waiver, you have been squeezed."

"Notice," continued Mustache earnestly, "that this excludes pseudo squeezes. It's not enough that having to discard is damaging, perhaps because you don't know which card to throw. We require that every possible discard is damaging on the actual layout."

Tush thought about this, but before he could make a rejoinder, Corky spoke up.

"Isn't there an issue with signaling? I mean, being allowed to refuse to play to a trick gives your side another communication option. You could use it to indicate no preference, for example, among unplayed suits. Then, if you're damaged by not having this extra message option—which might be pretty hard to determine—you'd have to say you've been squeezed, even though you've got lots of expendable cards to play."

Beard raised one of his bushy white eyebrows appreciatively. "Good point. I suppose one could make an exception regarding signaling, but it is a troublesome issue."

"I think we should stick with the definition," said Mustache. "One could imagine some situation where every discard available sends the wrong message. I don't know, maybe you have all big spots in the suit you want to discourage, and all small ones in the suit you like. Then, I think this could be a legitimate squeeze. A 'signal squeeze,' perhaps."

All four players sat lost in thought for some seconds.

"Maybe we'd better put off this discussion, and help these nice young folks move on to the second deal," said Beard. "Zero IMPs, right?"

TUSH IS CAUGHT IN A HOBSON'S SQUEEZE

Second in hand, Tush picked up

♠AJ109 ♡— ◇87653 ♣9762

and Mustache, to Tush's right, began with a big club, Ricochet. Beard responded 2◇, natural and positive; Mustache bid 2NT, raised by Beard. Mustache now bid 4♣, natural, eliciting a heart cuebid from his partner, and continued with 5NT, meaning "pick a slam." Beard chose 6◇. After two passes Tush doubled, hoping that partner's hand would help her find the heart lead, and that the opponents either didn't have or wouldn't find a profitable place to run.

However, after two passes East pulled to 6NT. Oh well, thought Tush, maybe they're short a trick in notrump.

The auction had been:

West	North	East	South
Beard	Corky	Mustache	Tush
		1♣	pass
2◇	pass	2NT	pass
3NT	pass	4♣	pass
4♡	pass	5NT	pass
6◇	pass	pass	dbl
pass	pass	6NT	all pass

Tush led a passive diamond. The full deal was:

Contract: 6NT by East
Opening lead: ◇8

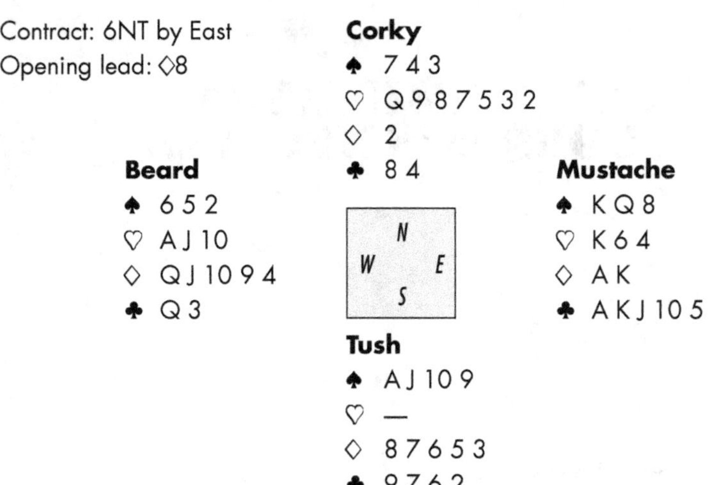

Corky
♠ 7 4 3
♡ Q 9 8 7 5 3 2
◇ 2
♣ 8 4

Beard
♠ 6 5 2
♡ A J 10
◇ Q J 10 9 4
♣ Q 3

Mustache
♠ K Q 8
♡ K 6 4
◇ A K
♣ A K J 10 5

Tush
♠ A J 10 9
♡ —
◇ 8 7 6 5 3
♣ 9 7 6 2

Declarer cashed the ◇A, ◇K, crossed to dummy's ♣Q, and cashed the rest of the diamonds, ditching all three of his spades. From this even dummy could see that only an overtrick was at issue. When Mustache continued by running the clubs, now discarding spades from the board, it became clear that the thirteenth trick depended on a heart guess. Tush's partner did her best by pitching hearts and spades alternately.

At the point when the last club was to be played, the hands had come down to:

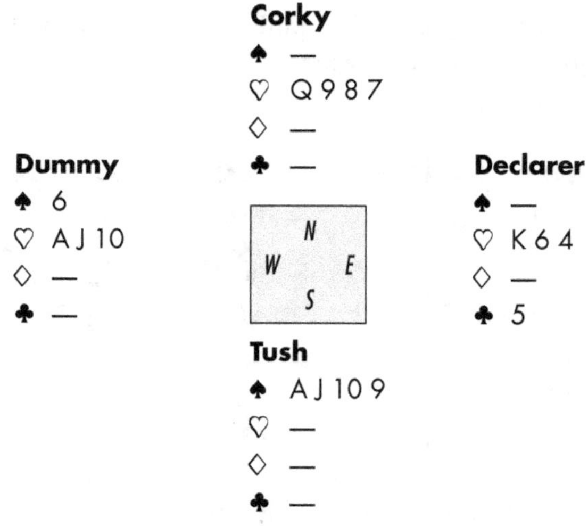

Corky
♠ —
♡ Q 9 8 7
◇ —
♣ —

Dummy
♠ 6
♡ A J 10
◇ —
♣ —

Declarer
♠ —
♡ K 6 4
◇ —
♣ 5

Tush
♠ A J 10 9
♡ —
◇ —
♣ —

There was a short hesitation before declarer cashed his last club with a triumphant look. Tush was down to ♠AJ109; he threw the nine.

Declarer pitched dummy's ♠6, played a heart to dummy's ace and took the now-marked finesse through Corky, making seven.

"Cute squeeze," said Beard. "A well-earned IMP."

"Thanks," said Mustache.

Tush looked right and left and even took an exaggerated peek under the table. "Was someone squeezed?" he inquired.

"You were," said Mustache cheerfully. "On the last club."

"You're kidding me, right?" said Tush. "I've heard of one-suit squeezes, but I had four equals in a dead suit. That would make it a one-card squeeze, and I don't think..."

"Nonetheless, it's a perfectly genuine squeeze," Beard interrupted. "Since you showed a void in the bidding, you had to be down to either four spades or four hearts. Your pitch on the last club would tell me which, guaranteeing my overtrick."

Tush thought about this. It did seem that having to discard on the last club forced him to reveal useful information. Again a non-material squeeze, but clearly worth half a trick here.

"Just a minute. Don't I have to have some sort of choice to be squeezed? If I do this, so-and-so happens, and if I do the other thing, some other bad thing happens."

"Sure," said Mustache. "Sometimes you have two choices, sometimes three, this time you had only one. 'Hobson's choice,' I think is what they call it."

Tush remembered reading about that phrase in grade school. Thomas Hobson was a stable master in Cambridge during the reign of Henry VIII, and the story was, you could spend all day describing the kind of horse you wanted but he always gave you the one nearest the door.

Tush decided, wisely, to be a good sport about it. "So, I guess we should call it a 'Hobson's squeeze,' then." Tush detected a subtle expression of relief on Corky's face.

But he couldn't leave well enough alone. "Come to think of it, wasn't my partner Hobson-squeezed as well? You can also tell from her discard which suit my void was in. A double Hobson's squeeze!"

East mumbled something about Tush having to play first, and the two professors got up to move for the next round.

But as they left, Tush knitted his eyebrows and made a subtle wipeout motion with his hands, indicating (he hoped) to Corky that he did not concede that he had been squeezed!

TUSH NEEDS AN ENCRYPTED SIGNAL

The next two opponents were a middle-aged couple, well-mannered but businesslike. They looked to Tush like they might be very strong players; had he seen them before at the Nationals, perhaps?

Tush was not prone to preempt at unfavorable vulnerability, but holding

♠ 10 8 3   ♡ A Q 10 7 6 5 4   ◇ J 10 5   ♣ —

as dealer, he could hardly be blamed for calling 3♡. Certainly, it couldn't be right to give these two a free ride in the bidding.

This was doubled by West (the woman), raised to 4♡ by Corky, and passed back around to West. Unfazed, West persisted with 4♠.

West	North	East	South
			3♡
dbl	4♡	pass	pass
4♠	all pass		

Corky led the ♡2.

Contract: 4♠ by West
Opening lead: ♡2

Dummy
♠ Q
♡ K 9 8
◇ 9 7 6 4
♣ 8 7 5 4 3

Tush
♠ 10 8 3
♡ A Q 10 7 6 5 4
◇ J 10 5
♣ —

Declarer put up dummy's ♡K, ruffed Tush's ace, and led a small trump to the queen. Tush was about to follow small when it hit him: this was a classic situation for a trump echo. His partner was likely to get in with a diamond at Trick 3, and a club ruff was beginning to look like it might be just the thing.

But declarer can also see the signal, thought Tush, and if she deduces that trumps are 3-3, she may decide to squander her table entry, return to hand safely and draw trumps. That would not be good for the defense.

But now, Tush had taken far too long. If he played low he had no way to win: declarer would wonder if he had been contemplating an echo, while partner would be barred from acting on the same deduction. So Tush dropped the ♠8.

The full deal in fact was:

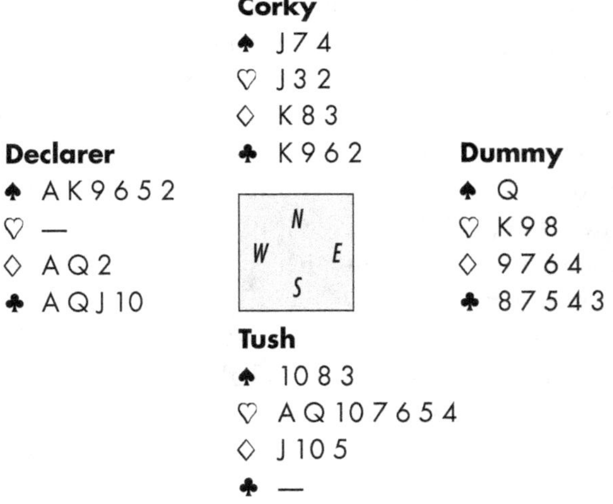

As Tush feared, declarer scrutinized his ♠8, ruffed a heart to hand and laid down high trumps. A few tricks later she was enjoying +420 and a hard-earned IMP against the par club game.

"Nothing I can do about it," said Tush to Corky. "Classic case of tell one, tell all. If I follow with the small trump, she hooks the diamond, but are you going to play a club now? I don't think so."

"Unfortunately, the encrypted signalers may be beating this one," said Corky. "When declarer ruffs the opening lead, the defenders know the whole heart-suit layout and declarer doesn't. This sets up a key for the defense, enabling them to encrypt the trump echo."

Tush was lost. "Encrypt the echo? What are you talking about?"

"Here's how my regular partner and I would do it," said Corky patiently. "Often, when you defend a trump contract, you lead your suit and declarer ruffs in at some point. At that moment, since the dummy is exposed and declarer is out of the suit, you and your partner know the exact distribution of every spot card. You now focus on the smallest spot card whose location the declarer can't deduce. That card becomes the 'key.' If leader has it, subsequent signaling is normal. Otherwise, all signals for the remainder of the play are upside-down.

"In the deal we just played, only you and I know who has the three of hearts. Since I have it, signaling is normal, and when trumps are led you echo with the eight. Declarer learns nothing, because you might be denying a trump echo if you happen to be the one holding the key card."

"This can't be legal," said Tush.

"As far as the laws of bridge are concerned, there's nothing illegal about it. If the opponents ask what your signal means, I tell them: either you have three trumps, interest in a ruff, and no three of hearts; or you have the heart three and no message. Assuming you had a choice, of course.

"Think of it as the card-play equivalent of the rotated asking bid we encountered before. It's perfectly okay that I can read your trump signal even though declarer can't; it's by virtue of my knowledge of the cards in my own hand.

"True, encrypted signaling is specifically banned by the ACBL for pairs play. Luckily, this club is more enlightened."

The opponents didn't seem to be expressing any surprise at these revelations. "Have you guys encountered this stuff before?" asked Tush.

"Oh yes, in fact we play it," said West.

"So you'd have beaten four spades, if you'd been North-South?"

"Sure, but not that way. I'd have doubled four spades with your hand, to get a club lead."

"Clear-cut," East agreed. "Ace and a void."

TUSH ENCOUNTERS AN ENCRYPTED LEAD

The next auction was brief: fourth in hand, Tush opened 1NT and was raised to three.

South	West	North	East
	pass	pass	pass
1NT	pass	3NT	all pass

The ♠3 was led.

Contract: 3NT by South
Opening lead: ♠3

Dummy
- ♠ Q J 10
- ♡ K Q 8
- ◇ Q 10 9 4
- ♣ 9 8 5

Tush
- ♠ A 2
- ♡ A 5 4
- ◇ J 8 6
- ♣ A K 10 6 2

Dummy's ♠10 held, East following with the six. This, thought Tush, was a classic. Since spades were apparently 4-4, he could just drive out the top diamonds and claim nine tricks.

Oops—there was a message for Tush on his table display:

```
ENCRYPTED LEADS AGAINST 3NT
4TH BEST FROM HANDS WITH 7+ POINTS,
OTHERWISE 3RD AND 5TH
```

Tush gave East a hard look. "Is there some theory that says odd leads work better from weak hands?"

"That's not the point. The hand playing three notrump is typically in a very limited high-card range, and dummy is exposed, so most of the time I can count my partner's points accurately enough to tell which kind of lead she made. But you can't."

Tush was beginning to see now why Corky was confident that he would see more "crypto" today. He could recall sessions where half the deals seem to have been played in 3NT.

Now, the problem at hand. If the lead was from five (likely, since with only four West would be more likely to have found a different lead) it would be better to play on clubs; the odds strongly favored having only one loser in that suit. And the spade length might even be with East.

Or should he cash one high club, and if nothing came down, revert to the diamond plan? That was safe enough, if spades were 4-4.

On the ♣A only small clubs appeared. Damn. Well, clubs were still by far the best bet. But when Tush crossed to the board with a heart and led the ♣9, East pitched a diamond.

Tush was now doomed to down two. At least, let the spades be 5-3, he prayed, but such was not to be:

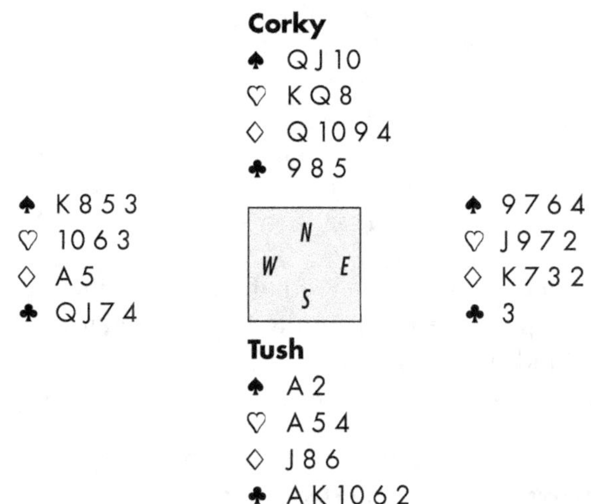

<pre>
                    Corky
                  ♠ Q J 10
                  ♡ K Q 8
                  ◇ Q 10 9 4
                  ♣ 9 8 5

   ♠ K 8 5 3   N   ♠ 9 7 6 4
   ♡ 10 6 3   ♡ J 9 7 2
   ◇ A 5   W   E   ◇ K 7 3 2
   ♣ Q J 7 4   S   ♣ 3

                    Tush
                  ♠ A 2
                  ♡ A 5 4
                  ◇ J 8 6
                  ♣ A K 10 6 2
</pre>

Par was +400 North-South. Nine easy tricks. Eleven IMPs away.

"I'd have done the same against an attitude lead," Tush said, unwilling to concede a point to the cryptologists. But he knew what the point was: East got a count on the spade suit, and Tush didn't.

TUSH CONSTRUCTS A ZERO PAR

Round 6 brought a couple of cheery gentlemen, who, if not actually inebriated, were clearly having a good time. "Corky!" cried one, "Ha' y' doin'? Who's yer podnuh?"

"This is Robert," said Corky. "He's new, be nice to him. Robert, this is James and Herbert."

The bidding on the first board was brief but, to Tush, quite surprising:

West	North	East	South
James	Corky	Herbert	Tush
pass	pass	pass	pass

The deal lit up on the table.

Corky
♠ 10 9 8 6
♡ K 9 7
◇ K J 5 3
♣ 9 3

James
♠ Q 7 3
♡ Q 6 4 2
◇ A 9 8 2
♣ K 2

Herbert
♠ K 5 4
♡ A 8 5 3
◇ Q 4
♣ Q J 7 6

Tush
♠ A J 2
♡ J 10
◇ 10 7 6
♣ A 10 8 5 4

Par was +110 East-West for making 2♡.

Tush examined the East hand carefully. "Wouldn't most folks open with that?"

"With what?" said Herbert, East. "Playing Ricochet, you need thirteen to fifteen to open one notrump, or at least a better twelve than this. One club is big, one diamond shows diamonds, one of a major shows five…"

"So all balanced hands are opened with one club or one notrump? I agree that's nice and simple, but don't you miss some games?"

"Nah, in fact I think it's better to keep quiet with twelve balanced and let the opposition try to find the high cards. With unbalanced hands it's another story, of course—then we open light, as long as we have at least an ace and a king. And it's really nice to have diamonds when you bid them; those Precision folks have trouble with that suit."

"Well, looks like it cost you three IMPs, this time," said Tush.

"Oh really?" James chimed in. "How do you bid these hands?"

Tush thought: 1♣, 1♡, 2♡, then maybe 2NT? "I suppose we might've gotten too high," he conceded.

"I'm pretty happy with our minus three IMPs," said James. "And now we have more time to spend talking system with you two!"

This remark was followed by an awkward period of silence.

"Um, I wonder," mused James, reduced to picking up the thread himself, "could it ever happen that par is zero? Nobody can make anything?"

"Well, let's see," said Tush. "You'd need to arrange it so the opening lead is a big advantage. Like being able to run tricks. Hmm…. who's got some paper? Does this club even believe in paper?"

"I didn't really need this," said Herbert, producing from a copious jacket pocket a daily calendar refill. He removed the cellophane and ripped off January 1, handing it to Tush. Tush scribbled the following deal on the reverse:

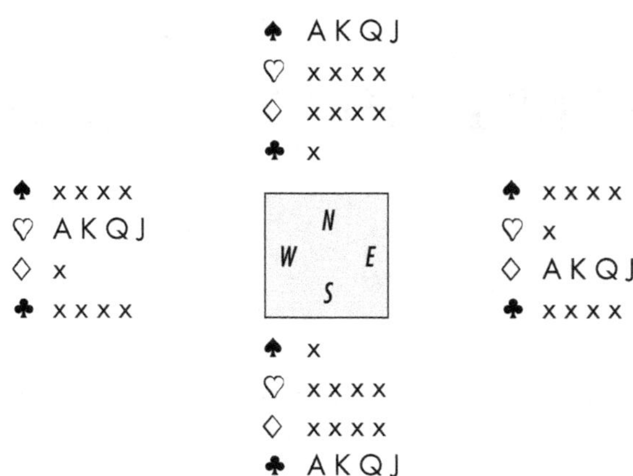

"East-West can run off eight tops against any contract by North-South, and vice-versa," Tush explained proudly.

"Not bad," James admitted. "I can't recall ever seeing a zero par in practice, though."

"Hey, listen," said Corky. "Maybe we should move on to the next board. Remember, P-G can terminate the round anytime he wants, and if everyone passes this board out, we could get caught short. Besides, who knows, maybe we'll take seven rounds of bidding on the next one."

EVERYBODY MAKES 3NT

Corky's prediction was about as far from the mark as possible: the bidding on Board 18 took no longer than the previous board's, and the play was over in the blink of an eye.

West	North	East	South
James	Corky	Herbert	Tush
		3NT	all pass

The table told Tush that the opening bid was

GAMBLING, NO SIDE ACE OR KING

Holding

♠ K Q J 4　♡ K J 6 2　♢ Q 7 2　♣ 5 4

Tush took no time to lead the ♠K.

As James put down

Dummy
♠　A 10
♡　A 8 4
♢　10 9 8 4 3
♣　9 6 3

he said: "Plus 400 for us."

Tush looked up. "Did I hear you right? Are you claiming *from dummy?*"

"He promised seven solid, nothing outside. Show him, Herbert."

Herbert exposed his cards:

♠ 9 6 5　♡ Q 3　◇ 5　♣ A K Q 10 8 7 2

They had indeed scored +400, which, Tush was gratified to see, was par. Apparently defensive ruffs could prevent North-South from scoring more than eight tricks in a major.

"Talk about the ideal hand to have when partner opens a gambling three notrump," remarked Corky. "Damn! Nineteen high-card points between the hands, and frigid."

"I suppose you could get down to fifteen high-card points," said Tush, still in construction mode. "You could give Herbert here ace, queen, jack nine times clubs and out, opposite James' hand. King has to drop, there's only one club out."

Herbert himself got into the act. "I don't see how you can do any better, unless, of course, you fix all four hands. Then, let me see, I think you can get it down to six points." Scribbling furiously on the back of another deposit slip, he presented:

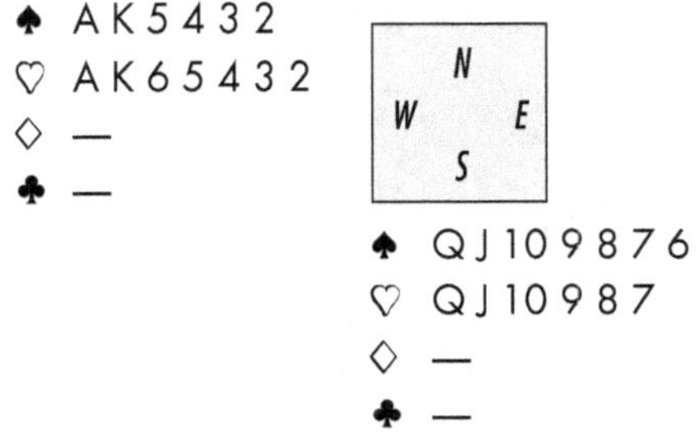

"South, with the quacks, makes three notrump. We give North a yarborough, of course, leaving East with a whale of an unusual notrump."

"We should be able to shave a point or two off of that," said Tush. "How about if we give East stiff jacks in the majors? Something like…. no, wait, that doesn't work. Then we have to give some minor-suit cards to South and West, which means either more winners to West or more losers to South."

"We could do something like this," said Corky, who had been writing on the back of January 2.

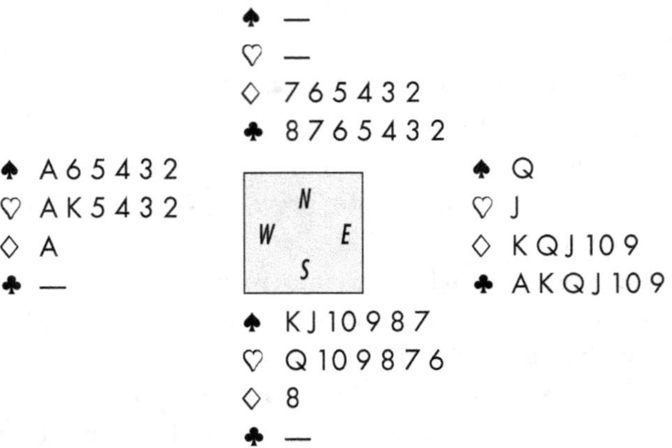

"Still six points, though. Damn."

In the meantime Tush had ripped off January 3. "How about this one? Again six points, but it makes three notrump from either end."

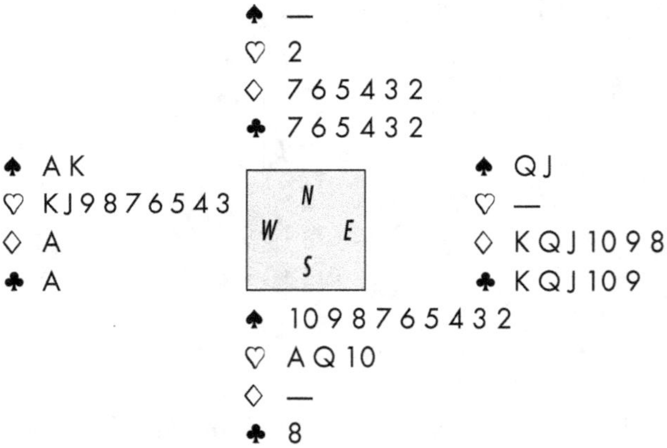

"I'm not sure that works," said James. "What do you pitch, as South, if the defense begins with West's two stiff aces?"

"Yipes! You're right. Squeezed at Trick 2. Shoot!"

"I guess we have our homework," said Herbert. "Give six points to North and South so both can make three notrump, and beat six points with a deal where only South is required to make it."

"Hey," said Tush, "have you seen this fantastic deal where everyone can make three notrump? Let me see if I can reconstruct it." Reaching again for the calendar, Tush scribbled for several minutes before he was ready to present.

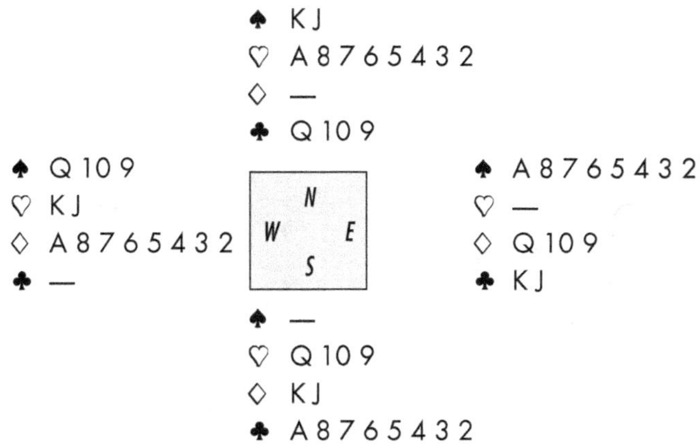

"You can assume it's three notrump by South; it's the same for everyone. If West leads diamonds, declarer pitches a club from dummy and then ducks a club. The defense's diamonds are blocked, so declarer makes seven clubs, a diamond and the ace of hearts. If the defense leads spades, declarer pitches a heart from hand and ducks a heart. Finally, if West leads a heart, declarer wins cheaply, cashes two more rounds, and then plays ace and another club to set up dummy, winding up with an overtrick."

"That really is sensational," said Corky. "Who could come up with something like that?"

"Some guy named Beasley, I think, but I remember reading that the same deal was found independently by computer." [1]

"By the way," said Corky, "do you guys know about the famous open question of whether you can construct a deal where North-South can make seven of any suit but not even five notrump?"

"I've seen a construction that doesn't make six," said James. "I think South is four-four-four-one with a stiff ace and tenaces."

"Here's another, where South really has to work to make five notrump."

---

1   More precise references for this and other arcana can be found in Notes and Sources at the end of this volume.

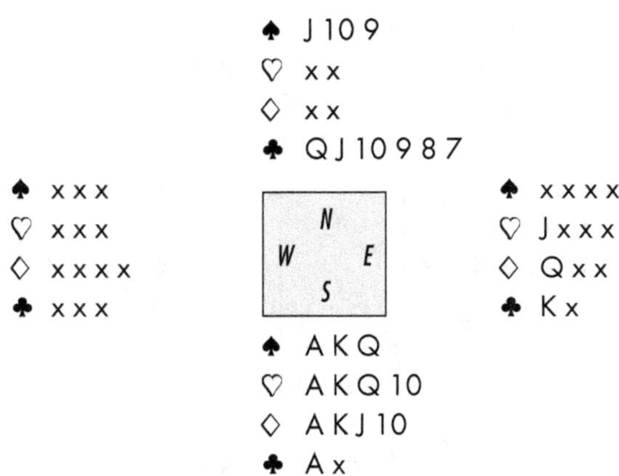

James looked over the deal carefully. "Hmm, I see, in notrump South has to knock out the queen of diamonds first, then run diamonds to make East let go a spade. Now he cashes the spades and gets his eleventh trick with a round suit endplay. But no one can improve the construction? Curious."

"As long as the round hasn't been called yet," Herbert put in, "here's one where the object is to get the least out of your resources. Construct North-South hands that have all forty high-card points and only mediocre play for six notrump."

But, just then, the table flashed

END OF ROUND 9

Saved by the bell.

TUSH BATTLES A TWO-SUITER

Two studious-looking young men—one white, one black—approached the table. The former greeted Corky and, as he settled in the West seat, offered his hand to Tush.

"I'm Simon," he said, with a slight accent Tush couldn't quite place, "and this is Kyle."

Tush introduced himself, thinking: college students? Could be tough. Shrugging, Tush picked up

♠ K 9 8 3   ♡ K 10   ◇ A Q 8   ♣ A 8 7 5

and opened 1NT as dealer.

After a pass by West, Corky bid 2◇. Tush was ready to accept the transfer when he saw that East had come in with a vulnerable 4♣ bid. The table offered no explanation, so Tush had to presume the call was natural. With four of East's suit and only two of partner's, a double seemed in order, but Tush steeled himself to make a disciplined pass. After all, partner had shown nothing and the opponents knew they were vulnerable.

This rode around to Corky, who came back in with 4◇. Uh-oh, thought Tush: was this natural, or a re-transfer? Surely, Yellow Card would say natural, but perhaps logic should take preference? Well, Tush was within his rights to correct to four hearts in any case.

He never got the chance: East was in there again, this time with a 4♠ call.

"Double," said Tush out loud, then instantly turned crimson. "Oops, I'm sorry, I didn't mean that, um, no, I did mean that, I just forgot…"

"It's okay, relax," said West. "Just enter your call on the table."

Tush did as suggested but realizing, with a sinking feeling, that Corky was now going to have to pull his double with any hand that could remotely justify that action. Unless the computer had given her a chance to commit to sitting for a double?

But West made it moot by correcting to 5♣, passed to Tush. The auction so far had been:

West	North	East	South
Simon	Corky	Kyle	Tush
			1NT
pass	2◇	4♣	pass
pass	4◇	4♠	dbl
5♣	pass	pass	?

It was obvious to double this, despite Corky's implicit invitation to bid on. He'd nearly doubled 4♣. But to be bidding like this vulnerable, East must be either nuts or the possessor of a freak hand, and he looked pretty sane. It was now clear that Corky must have a red two-suiter, and Tush had some golden cards for her. 5◇ could make or be a cheap save.

On the other hand, bad breaks were looming. And those black spots beckoned. Nervously, Tush doubled. Everyone passed and he led the ◇A.

Contract: 5♣ doubled, by East
Opening lead: ◇A

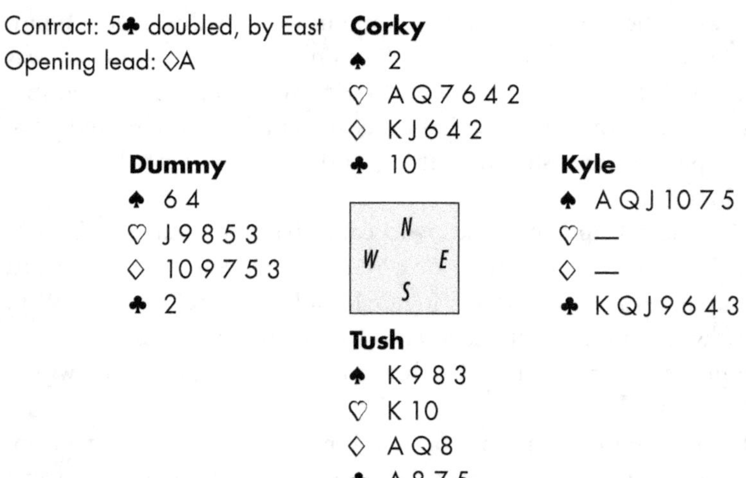

The play took less than a minute. Declarer ruffed the opening lead, then accepted two more forces as he knocked out the ♣A, drew trump, and gave up a trick to the ♠K. The ♣QJ9 drew the remaining trumps and East ran his good spades for +750, 14 IMPs.

Par was +200 N-S, for beating 6♣ doubled by one; both 5◇ and 5♡ were makeable, Tush noted. 4♠ by East, however, was not. Kudos to West for his preference on a stiff deuce; not a bid Tush would have found.

East turned sympathetically to Tush. "I saw that you thought about bidding on," he said. "You have good table feel. I think I'd have doubled without even thinking."

"It occurred to me that you might be all black," said Tush. "Um, that is, that your hand was all black. Your bridge hand." Out of the corner of his eye, Tush could see Corky hiding her face behind her cards. "I guess we should call that an African-American hand, right?" This with a feeble attempt at laughter.

East turned to his partner. "I don't get it."

"He thinks you're African-American," explained West. "Actually," turning to Tush, "I'm the African-American."

Tush stared uncomprehendingly.

"Born and bred in Bloemfontein, South Africa," said West. "Got my U.S. citizenship only last year."

"I understand, but he's…"

"Cleveland, Ohio," said East cheerily. "I'm a native American."

TUSH MAKES HIS OWN DOUBLED CONTRACT

Holding

♠ A Q 10   ♡ A 10 8 7 5   ◇ 8 6   ♣ A 8 6

fourth in hand, both sides vulnerable, Tush watched as two passes were followed by a 1♠ opening on his right. More words appeared in front of Tush:

```
RICOCHET: 5+ SPADES, 11-15 HCP
```

So they were Ricochet players. What to do now? The hearts were meagre, but the spade holding looked like a triple stopper, so Tush stretched to make a 1NT overcall.

On Tush's left, the South African reached out to push his double button. This was passed around to Tush, who pulled nervously to 2♡. West doubled once more, and all passed.

The bidding had been:

West	North	East	South
Simon	Corky	Kyle	Tush
pass	pass	1♠	1NT
dbl	pass	pass	2♡
dbl	all pass		

The ♠9 was led and dummy came down.

Contract: 2♡ doubled, by South
Opening lead: ♠9

Dummy
♠ 5 4 2
♡ Q J 4
◊ 9 5 4
♣ 7 5 4 2

Tush
♠ A Q 10
♡ A 10 8 7 5
◊ 8 6
♣ A 8 6

Tush marvelled at the nice trumps in dummy. Four trump tricks, three spades and the ♣A—he could make this! That would be sweet revenge for the last board.

Winning East's ♣K with the ace, Tush fingered a small trump in hand. Let's see, trump to the board; if it holds, hook the spades and draw trumps. Otherwise, get to the board next time and do the same.

Any glitches? Hmm, yes—a spade ruff by West. Hopefully West has another spade, thought Tush, but if he also has king fourth of trumps—likely—he can duck the first trump. Then after Tush takes the spade finesse, he can get in with the trump king, put his partner in with a diamond and sink Tush's ship with a spade ruff.

Plunking down the ♡A first didn't seem to help; same problem. It looked like Tush would have to lead a trump toward dummy, return to hand with a club, and lead a second trump toward dummy.

Better check that through once more—there are lots of IMPs riding on this! Releasing the ♣A was dangerous; if West had a doubleton club he could get a trump promotion. Even easier, he could pitch his spade on East's good club and ruff a spade after all. Shoot.

If there were only a way to underlead in trumps and still keep the table's trump entry if West ducked—but of course, there was! Brightening, Tush finally led to Trick 2: and it was the ♡10 that hit the table.

The full deal:

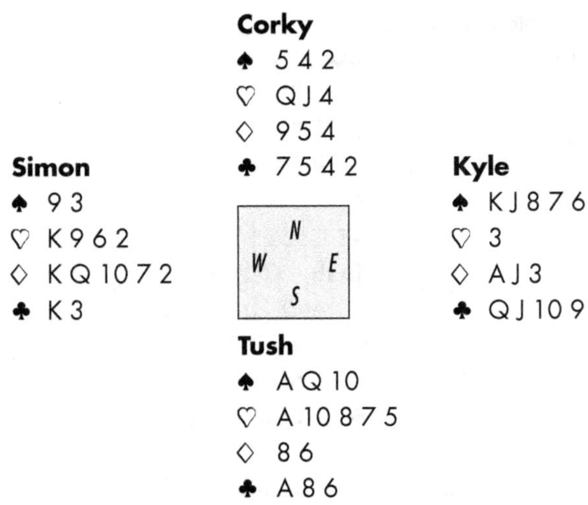

Simon was helpless. He let the ♡10 hold, and rose with his king on the small trump that followed. But nothing could prevent Tush from reaching dummy with the third round of trumps, finessing in spades, and drawing the last trump from hand. That was +670 for North-South, 13 IMPs against par (+110 East-West for a partial in spades or diamonds).

"Sorry about that," said Simon to East.

"No, my fault," said Kyle generously. "I bid for that spade lead."

Trying to figure out how he could politely call attention to his own brilliant play, Tush started to say something about how the contract would usually go down. Fortunately for Tush, Simon had been studying the table display, and now said: "That ten of hearts was a nice play."

Tush beamed modestly, if such a thing was possible. He was sharp tonight, no doubt about it. Good things were going to happen.

TUSH PITCHES THE WRONG CARD

A largish, scowling man of about forty-five lowered himself into the West chair. "My partner's coming, I think. Sorry, she's been in a bit of a tizzy all day."

A short time later a woman arrived, snapping her purse closed as she sat.

Corky was the dealer; her opening bid of 1♠ was undisturbed by East. With

♠2　♡Q 10 8 7 3 2　◇8 6　♣6 5 3 2

Tush passed, hoping to be able to back in with hearts later.

West reopened with 2NT, flashed as UNUSUAL on the table in front of Tush. Indeed it is, thought Tush. Didn't most people play a re-opening 2NT as natural? The rest of the auction sounded natural enough:

West	North	East	South
	1♠	pass	pass
2NT	pass	3NT	all pass

Corky took a few seconds to find a lead, Tush projecting "Hearts! Hearts!" with all the force of mental waves he could muster. Yes! Jack of hearts! It worked! Oops, no—what hit the table was a most unexpected jack of *diamonds*.

The appearance of dummy helped to explain the opening lead, but what could explain the dummy itself?

Contract: 3NT by West
Opening lead: ◇J

Dummy
♠ A K Q J 10 9 8
♡ 9 6 5 4
◇ 3
♣ Q

Tush
♠ 2
♡ Q 10 8 7 3 2
◇ 8 6
♣ 6 5 3 2

Declarer's first response to the apparition laid out before him was to take off and clean his glasses. But dummy was still there. "You're kidding me, right? Where's your real hand?"

"What, you don't like my spade stopper?"

West sighed and finally won the lead in hand with the ◇Q. A club went to Corky's king; Corky's ◇10 to declarer's king; declarer's ♣J to Corky's ace, and Corky's ◇9 to declarer's ace. On this card Tush chucked his deuce of spades, thinking that Corky might appreciate confirmation that the thirteenth spade was not in declarer's hand.

Declarer had been pitching spades from the board, from the ace down, in a manner suggesting that his primary purpose was to irritate his partner. He now ran his four good clubs, pitching the rest of dummy's spades. After this, Tush and the dummy were down to four hearts each: ♡9654 on the board, ♡Q1087 in Tush's hand. Declarer played the ♡A, dropping Corky's king, then the jack to Tush's queen. Tush cashed the ♡10 but the board took Trick 13 with the ♡9. Making three.

"I knew you'd find a way to get to my hand," said dummy brightly.

The full deal lit up on the table.

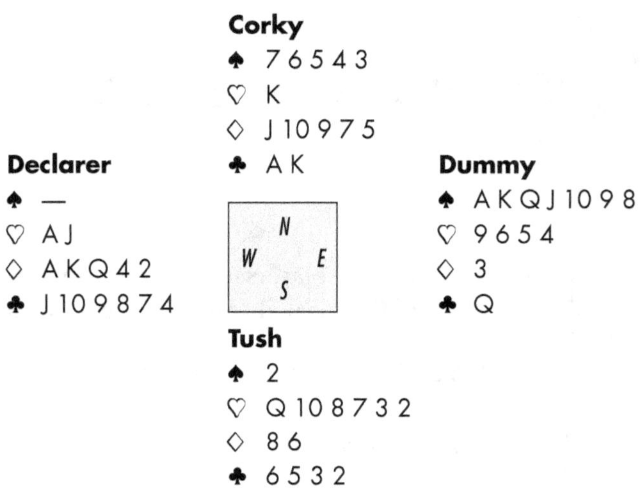

"I think if you happen to hold on to your spade I go down," said West to Tush.

Tush studied the board. Indeed, it did look as though if he had clung to the ♠2, the dummy would have been strip-squeezed. Forced to keep all dummy's hearts, declarer would have had to choose between unguarding the seven-times-stopped spades, or—if he abandoned club winners in his hand—seeing the board thrown in with a spade to lead away from the ♡9. But no: "You can always make the hand by cashing the ace of hearts and throwing my partner in with a diamond."

"You're missing the point. It's important for the future of the partnership that my partner's spades not take any tricks."

For a few seconds, no one spoke.

"I always find it's a good idea to keep a card in my partner's suit," said the dummy sweetly to Tush.

This was too much for Tush. "My partner's suit?" he sputtered. "You call that my partner's suit? If I don't lead a heart, you have a slam in that suit!"

Par was 450 to East-West for the spade game, so two IMPs would accrue to Corky and Tush. "Well, I got us to game," said East to her partner. "Of course, if you reopen with a double, we can get a telephone number."

"Oh, right," said West with heavy sarcasm. "It's my fault we play in three notrump with seven winners on the moon."

Another few seconds ticked by, then, Tush to Corky: "Did you really have to open that hand?"

"Jesus!" said Corky. "A near-par result, and no one is happy!"

TUSH FINDS AN EXIT

It took a few minutes for all four players to calm down and pick up their hands for the next board. East passed as dealer and Tush, looking at

♠ 8 6 5   ♡ A 6   ◇ A J 4   ♣ Q 10 7 4 2

was not inclined to open. The auction proceeded:

West	North	East	South
		pass	pass
1NT	pass	2◇	pass
2♡	pass	2NT	pass
3♠	pass	4♠	all pass

The 1NT opening was 15-17, the response a transfer, the rest natural. Corky led the ◇K.

Contract: 4♠ by West
Opening lead: ◇K

Corky
♠ J 9
♡ 10 5 4 2
◇ K Q 10 6 2
♣ 9 6

Declarer
♠ A K Q 10 3
♡ 8 7
◇ 8 7 3
♣ A K 5

Dummy
♠ 7 4 2
♡ K Q J 9 3
◇ 9 5
♣ J 8 3

Tush
♠ 8 6 5
♡ A 6
◇ A J 4
♣ Q 10 7 4 2

Declarer paused to study dummy, and Tush made himself relax and think. The bidding, together with Corky's lead, made West's hand pretty much an open book. He had to have the top clubs and probably the top three spades as well, and since he bypassed 3♡, a doubleton there. And thus, presumably, 5–2–3–3 distribution.

It was too late to prevent a diamond ruff, so declarer had ten tricks. But maybe Tush could keep him from enjoying a second heart trick. Let's see: lead overtaken, trump, diamond, trump, diamond ruffed, club back to declarer's hand, last trump drawn, heart ducked. Oops, that wouldn't work: another heart and Tush would be endplayed, forced to lead away from his ♣Q.

So, thought Tush, maybe I need to play ace and another heart, to kill the dummy and simultaneously scuttle the endplay. Wait, no: declarer would play a third heart, intending to ditch his club loser. Tush could ruff this but then an overruff, followed by a late diamond ruff on the board, would leave Tush unable to ruff the board's good hearts.

Rats. Maybe the best hope was to overtake the lead and play a highish club, trying to convince declarer that the queen was on his left. Tush was about to do this when another idea struck. With the beginnings of a smile on his lips, Tush overtook with the ♢A and led a *small* heart.

West was stymied. What could he do? Finally he won on the board (with the jack over Corky's ten) and led a diamond. But Tush was careful to go in with the jack—Corky following low—and cash the ♡A before exiting in trumps.

Declarer could do no better than win in hand, draw a second round of trump, take his diamond ruff and try to cash a heart. When Tush ruffed he overruffed, but had to concede a club at Trick 13. That was +100 to Tush and Corky, 6 IMPs against the –140 par for 3♡ or 3♠ by East-West.

"No way to make it," West said to his partner. "Short hearts with the long trump." Not even a glance in Tush's direction.

Corky, however, seemed to appreciate Tush's defense. "I could have led a trump, I suppose," she offered, "but you made a nice recovery. I can see that he makes on an endplay if you lead back trumps."

Tush beamed. Making the right play made him feel tingly all over. And the approving look on Corky's face—that, thought Tush, if captured, could be used to revive heart-attack victims.

TUSH DEFENDS IN THE DARK

Two silver-haired ladies took their seats East-West. Corky exchanged friendly hellos with them, then: "Robert, this is Harriet and Lee Ann. They're the club's senior Ricochet players, I think, yes?"

"That's a nice way to put it, dearie," said West, Harriet. And to Tush: "Very pleased to meet you."

"Likewise," said Tush, waving tentatively to each opponent with his right hand as he extracted his cards with his left. With a not-too-thrilling

♠ 7 6 5 2   ♡ Q J 5   ◇ A 6 4   ♣ 10 6 3

he passed as dealer.

Harriet began with 1♠ (Ricochet: 5+ spades, 11-15 HCP), Corky passed, and Lee Ann's 1NT response was alerted by the table display as ARTIFICIAL AND STRONG. The auction proceeded:

West	North	East	South
Harriet	Corky	Lee Ann	Tush
			pass
1♠	pass	1NT	pass
2◇	pass	2♡	pass
3♣	pass	3NT	all pass

Responder's 2♡ had been alerted as waiting for description. Lee Ann volunteered that her partner was probably 5–1–4–3 on this bidding.

What to lead? The ♡Q looked obvious, but Tush was uncomfortably aware that East was likely to have long hearts, having settled for notrump only after finding partner with at most a stiff. Though fairly safe, the heart lead could cost a vital tempo. On the other hand, the minors hardly looked promising, and if a spade was right, this game was too tough for Tush.

So Tush extracted a reluctant ♡Q and the dummy came down.

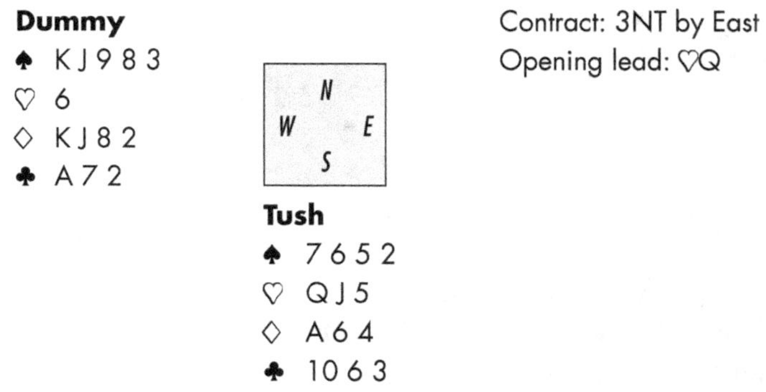

The ♡Q collected the six, eight and nine. Now what? Where were the small heart spots? Could declarer have had an original holding of ♡A1097432? If so, continuing with the jack would bring down partner's king, too horrible to contemplate. But surely Corky would have overtaken with king doubleton.

On the other hand, maybe declarer had only ♡A109, and continuing the suit would set up five heart tricks to go with Corky's presumed spade entry. Nah, surely East would have found some other contract with that holding.

Tush's head hurt. This was ridiculous, how was he supposed to defend when he couldn't even guess declarer's length to within three cards? What decided it for him finally was that if he didn't play the ♡J, he'd have to choose among alternatives, and he just wasn't up to it.

In fact, the layout was fortunate for Tush.

Corky
♠ A 10
♡ 10 8 7 4 3 2
♦ 7 3
♣ Q 9 5

Harriet
♠ K J 9 8 3
♡ 6
♦ K J 8 2
♣ A 7 2

Lee Ann
♠ Q 4
♡ A K 9
♦ Q 10 9 5
♣ K J 8 4

Tush
♠ 7 6 5 2
♡ Q J 5
♦ A 6 4
♣ 10 6 3

The ♡J drew a diamond from the board, ♡2 from partner, ace from declarer. Declarer had been thinking too, and swiftly played a spade to dummy's jack—and Corky's ten.

Forcing himself to look casual, Tush tried to figure out what the ♠10 meant. Had declarer underled her ♠AQx? Was Corky playing a deep game with ♠Q10, or, horrors, ♠AQ10? Wait, no, she must be ducking with ♠A10 to preserve the entry to her hearts. Would it work?

Lee Ann stared at this card. Her plan had been to steal a spade trick (if South had the ♠A) and revert to diamonds, then either finesse in clubs or—if hearts appeared to be 3-6—drive out South's ♠A. But if *North* had the ♠A, she'd want to knock it out now. Deciding that the odds favored sticking with her original line, she plunked down the ♦K.

Tush won and drove out the ♡K, while a club was pitched from the board. On the diamonds he and dummy each discarded a spade while Corky threw a club and a heart.

Declarer needed three more tricks in this position:

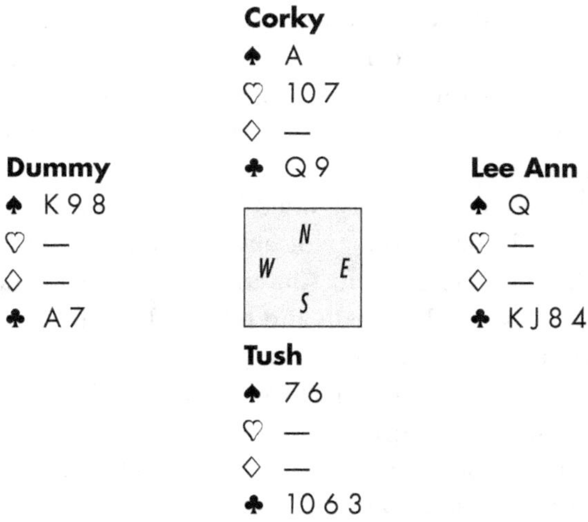

No need to risk the club finesse now, thought Lee Ann; even if South had held four hearts originally, there was only one to cash. So she led her ♠Q, overtaking with dummy's king, only to find that it was North, after all, who had held up the ace. Down one, –100 E–W against par of +630.

Tush glanced appreciatively at Corky, but before he could say anything, Lee Ann put up her hands in a gesture of helplessness. "Great defense," she said. "But, there must be a million ways to make this hand; I seem to have found the only one that goes down."

Harriet was sympathetic. "I suppose you could play on clubs first, counting on the finesse, then decide whether to go after spades or diamonds based on whether you get three club tricks or four."

"I thought of that, but if I turn out to need spades, I'd have burned my entry."

"Hmm, good point. How about this: in the end position, if you think hearts were three-six, you could cash the ace-king of clubs before leading spades? This lets you take advantage of Corky having been squeezed, as the cards lie."

An awkward silence followed this observation.

"I have a question about the bidding," Tush said to Lee Ann. "With that hand, you pretty much know you want to play in three notrump as soon as you hear the opening bid. Why do all that relaying? Doesn't that reveal unnecessary information to the opponents?"

Relieved to be off the topic of cardplay, Lee Ann responded animatedly. "Just the opposite! Think about it. Announcing that my hand wants to play three notrump opposite any one spade opener limits it severely. You were worried that I might have long hearts, right? When I run through the relays, you have no idea what I have. Of course, you hear about the dummy, but who cares? You see it anyway after the opening lead.

"Lots of people have the misguided idea that jumping to the final contract conceals information. Not always true. Sometimes longer auctions are less revealing. And sometimes, when you stay low, the opponents themselves will come in and tell you how to play the hand.

"Rule of thumb: when you and your partner have lots of high cards and no big fit, bid slow—especially if you know you will be the declarer, and it's partner who's doing the describing. You may not remember this, but it used to be standard that a direct jump to three notrump in response to a one-of-a-suit opener showed sixteen to seventeen points and 4-3-3-3 distribution—with three in partner's suit. What a crock! That bid was so blatantly bad that people stopped using it even before they had a replacement meaning."

"We use it to show a forcing raise with two of the top three trumps," contributed Harriet.

"Actually," continued Lee Ann, still playing her own ball, "the standard weak one notrump response to an opening bid is even worse than the three notrump response, since, first of all, you need it so strong hands can grab the denomination, and, secondly, it's the weak hands that need to show their suits immediately. It's the same theory as negative free bids, really, but it applies even more strongly when the opponents have not interfered.

"How often do you hold some random collection, something like,

$$\spadesuit x \quad \heartsuit K x x \quad \diamondsuit x x x \quad \clubsuit A Q x x x x$$

and it goes one spade, pass, to you? You want to bid two clubs, right? Of course you do! If you don't, you may never get the chance. But, turn two of your baby diamonds into the ace and queen, and now you're in no rush. Stay low, hear what partner has to say.

"Can you believe, two-over-one responses have gotten stronger over the years? Forcing to game? How... how... antediluvian!"

Despite recalling that the requirements for a 2/1 had cost him a bushel of IMPs back on Board 9, Tush felt compelled to put up some defense. "Now, wait a minute. Strong two-over-one responses have been developed over years of experience; they're time-tested and are a great foundation for finding the right game or slam."

Lee Ann scoffed. "They were developed over years, all right, years of non-interference by the opponents and archaic slam-bidding. Things have changed. You have to get in there with your suits when you're weak, and slow down when you're strong. You have to have a notion of captaincy. You have to have ways to get the unknown hand to be declarer. You need principles! You need ideas! You need experiments! You need..."

"Hey, hey, easy does it," said Harriet. "This young man"—gesturing toward Tush—"has grown up with the old ways. It'll take some time to get him to see the light."

"In the meantime," said Corky—whose presence had been forgotten for some time—"it's twelve IMPs for us old fogies, right?"

TUSH PLAYS FROM THE WRONG SIDE

For the next deal it was Corky who opened 1♠ in second position. Lee Ann passed, and Tush, with

♠ K J ♡ 7 6 4 2 ◇ Q 10 6 5 ♣ J 5 2

was happy to be able to bid a standard forcing 1NT. Corky raised to 3NT, and after some thought, Harriet led the ♣Q.

West	North	East	South
Harriet	*Corky*	*Lee Ann*	*Tush*
pass	1♠	pass	1NT
pass	3NT	all pass	

Contract: 3NT by South
Opening lead: ♣Q

Dummy
- ♠ A Q 10 9 6
- ♡ A Q 5
- ◇ A J
- ♣ K 7 3

Tush
- ♠ K J
- ♡ 7 6 4 2
- ◇ Q 10 6 5
- ♣ J 5 2

Tush looked askance at the lead; no explanation was forthcoming from the table. Should he cover or not? Could it be from queen doubleton? Maybe, but then it wouldn't matter what he did. Could it be from ace–queen fifth? Not a bad lead, Tush supposed, when the king was likely to be in dummy. If Tush covered in *that* case, he'd have to guess well for which red king to finesse West, because otherwise a club would come whistling through to set the contract.

So it must be right to duck. This Tush did, East following with the
♣6. West had apparently been using the time well, too, because she
now switched to the ♡J.

Reprieved in clubs, Tush now had to make something of the red
suits, so it seemed like a good time to try the ♡Q from the board. This
lost to the king, alas, and the ♡8 was returned to West's nine.

Well, thought Tush, the ♡K was wrong, but it looked like the
suit was 3-3. That would give him two hearts to go along with his five
spade tricks, ◇A and eventual club; good enough. So Tush ducked in
dummy.

West thought some more, annoying Tush. What has she got to
think about now? Tush found out soon enough: Harriet switched once
more, this time to the ◇4!

A silent expletive formed on Tush's lips. They were threatening to
set up their fifth defensive trick, *in Tush's suit*, before he could set up
his ninth offensive trick, in theirs! Tush had no choice but to insert the
◇J and pray.

For a few seconds, he thought his prayers had been heard. Lee
Ann, bewildered by her partner's switches, alternately blinked and
scratched her head. Finally she won the ◇K and led back a club. Down
one.

The full deal lit up on the table.

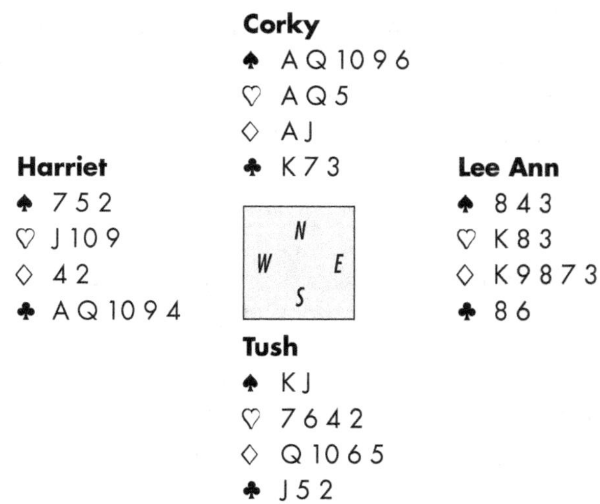

<pre>
                         Corky
                         ♠ A Q 10 9 6
                         ♡ A Q 5
                         ◇ A J
     Harriet   ♣ K 7 3   Lee Ann
     ♠ 7 5 2   ♠ 8 4 3
     ♡ J 10 9   N   ♡ K 8 3
     ◇ 4 2   W   E   ◇ K 9 8 7 3
     ♣ A Q 10 9 4   S   ♣ 8 6
                         Tush
                         ♠ K J
                         ♡ 7 6 4 2
                         ◇ Q 10 6 5
                         ♣ J 5 2
</pre>

Par was +400 to North-South, which, too late, Tush realized he could
have achieved if he had not squandered the ♡Q at Trick 2. Shrugging
off the 10 IMP loss, Tush addressed the Ricochet-fanatical Lee Ann.

"I'll grant you that my one notrump response did not work out well on this occasion," he conceded, "but what, exactly, would you have done with my hand if your partner had opened one spade?"

"No problem," said Lee Ann. "I just raise to two spades. Only guarantees two-card support."

"Really? And you make the same raise with four trumps and genuine offense?"

"Actually, no, with four trumps, and even with three and a singleton—especially if partner's suit is hearts—we jump to three, preemptive. Same as if right-hand opponent had doubled. That's a Ricochet principle, you know. Bid the same way with or without interference."

Tush thought about that raise scheme. Yes, he did feel that raising partner's 1♡ opener to two with

♠x ♡Qxx ◇Kxxx ♣Jxxxx

or the like was pissing in the wind, these days; opponents would brush that aside every time. From the other side, he could recall cheerfully reopening after the opposition had bid 1♠–2♠, whereas if that raise could have been made on a doubleton, he'd have had to think twice.

"It still seems to me," pursued Tush, "that you're going to bid a lot of hands to the wrong strain, by raising on a doubleton."

"Perhaps," said Lee Ann, gathering up her stuff. "Mostly for low-level stuff, of course, since our one-bids are limited. But the opponents hate it; they never know when they're rescuing us from a bad fit. Brings us a lot of IMPs. And us old ladies, we *love* them IMPs!"

X X X

Harriet and Lee Ann were replaced by three people—no, only two: an elderly couple, both short and plump, the woman dragging an enormous carpetbag. "Don't you just adore defending three notrump with the strong hand on the board?" said the woman to her partner. "That was such fun!"

Tush couldn't resist. "You guys beat three notrump?"

"Sure did! Harold led the jack of hearts. Declarer went up ace and I followed with the three—why tell him where the king is? Anyway, declarer played ace and jack of diamonds, which I ducked, of course. Then he crossed to a spade and played the queen of diamonds, club pitch by Harold, club pitch from the board, king by me. Now it was obvious to return a spade.

"The look on poor declarer's face was priceless. He'd worked so hard to set up a diamond trick, and now he realized that if he cashed it, he'd squeeze dummy and set up a trick for the defense! Here's what he was looking at." The woman extracted a pad and pencil from a compartment in her bag, and lettered neatly:

♠ A Q 10
♡ Q x
◇ —
♣ K x

[____________]

♠ —
♡ x x x
◇ 10
♣ J x x

"His only chance was to abandon the diamond winner and guess which suit would get him back to the board. I loved watching him suffer. Finally he led a heart to the queen and king. I returned a heart to Harold's ten and he got out with a spade, and the board was endplayed."

Tush was amazed at the disparity between the two successful defenses: clubs, hearts and diamonds at his table, spades at the other. Now, if they could just start play before anyone asked an embarrassing question.

"I suppose," asked Harold, "that you two wrapped up the game?"

Before Tush could say anything, Corky came to his rescue.

"We had no chance," she shrugged. "They ran off the first five tricks."

TUSH IS STUNG BY A ROTATED CUEBID

"My name is Mildred, and I guess you've figured out that this is Harold. You're Corky, right? But I don't think I've seen your partner here before."

"No, I'm new. Robert."

"Pleestameetcha," said Harold.

"That's quite a bag you've got there, Mildred," remarked Corky.

"Oh! I have to show you my latest Bridge Maxim!" With that, Mildred stuffed her pad and pencil back into the carpetbag and extracted a large rectangular frame, upon which stretched a partly-completed needlepoint design:

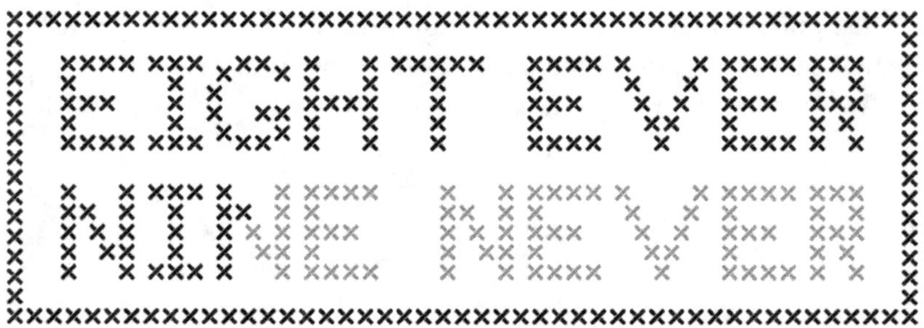

"Just your basic cross-stitch," said Mildred modestly, batting her eyelashes. "I also have 'COVER AN HONOR WITH AN HONOR', 'SECOND HAND LOW', 'THIRD—' "

"Ahem, Mildred," said Harold, looking at her over the top of his glasses, and gesturing to indicate that Corky had already passed as dealer.

"Sorry." Mildred put the frame away and extracted her cards. She took several seconds to sort them, then a few more to type in 1◇ on her display. Sitting quietly with

♠J854 ♡J652 ◇76 ♣QJ5

Tush witnessed the following auction.

West	North	East	South
Harold	Corky	Mildred	Tush
	pass	1◇	pass
2NT	pass	3♣	pass
4♣	pass	4♠	pass
5◇	pass	6◇	all pass

Tush's table display told him that 1◇ was Ricochet, at least four and usually 5+ diamonds, 11-15 HCP. The 2NT was a good limit raise or better, with one of the top three trumps; 3♣ confirmed the other two trump tops but was otherwise neutral; 4♣ and 4♠ were "rotated cuebids."

Tush, on lead against the slam, turned to West. "So three clubs means she has nothing special, but does have two out of the ace–king–queen of diamonds?"

"Right. We could actually stop in three diamonds after that."

"But"—this to East—"your partner is interested in slam anyway?"

"Yes, he must have a very nice hand. The suit he's cuebidding depends on which diamond top he has."

"Wait, let me guess. 'Ace is honest,' right? So if he has the ace of diamonds, he showed a first-round club control?"

"That's right! Very good, young man."

"And, let's see, 'king lies over,' so if his top diamond is the king, he was actually cuebidding spades?"

"Right again. And if it's the queen, his cuebid was for hearts. Of course, I can tell from my diamond holding which suit he cuebid, but you can't. Ta-da!"

"Okay. Now, you made a return cuebid of four spades, right? That's rotated the same way?"

"Exactly—according to the diamond top that's by itself. And we cue up the line, so Harold can infer that I'm missing a control."

Right, thought Tush, and now I get to find the killing lead, without knowing where their weakness is. Well, it won't be a trump this time. Nor will it be a club, because Corky had a chance to double that suit. So the best shot has to be one of the majors. Eeny meeny miny moe, catch a tiger by the toe… out came a spade, and down came the dummy.

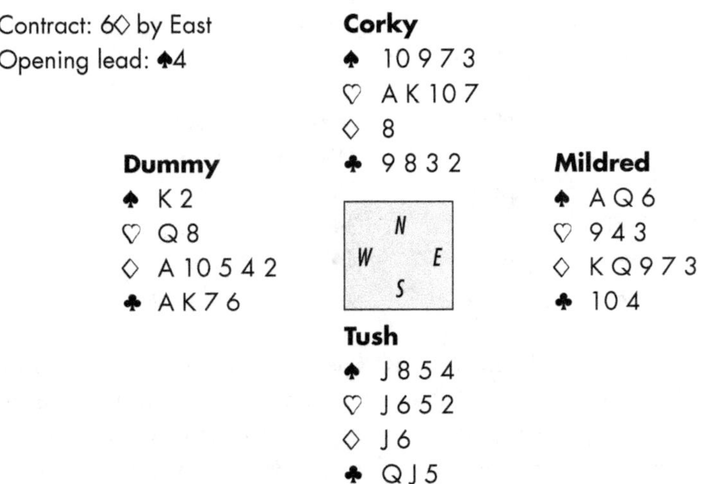

Contract: 6◇ by East
Opening lead: ♠4

Corky
- ♠ 10 9 7 3
- ♡ A K 10 7
- ◇ 8
- ♣ 9 8 3 2

Dummy
- ♠ K 2
- ♡ Q 8
- ◇ A 10 5 4 2
- ♣ A K 7 6

Mildred
- ♠ A Q 6
- ♡ 9 4 3
- ◇ K Q 9 7 3
- ♣ 10 4

Tush
- ♠ J 8 5 4
- ♡ J 6 5 2
- ◇ J 6
- ♣ Q J 5

The play took less than a minute. Declarer drew trump, threw a heart from dummy on her third spade, and claimed, conceding a heart. That was +1370 to East-West, versus par of +600 for game in diamonds or notrump. Minus 13 painful IMPs for Tush and Corky.

Sighing, Corky entered the score.

"Mildred… may I call you Mildred?" said Tush.

"Of course."

"Since the ace of diamonds was the lone trump top, all the cuebidding was 'honest,' yes?"

"Mm-hmm."

"So Harold showed the ace of clubs, then you showed the ace of spades but no first-round heart control, right?"

"That's right."

"Then armed with that information, Harold placed you in game."

"Right."

"And you have no second-round heart control."

"Right."

"So why did you bid the slam?"

"Why, because of the Fundamental Theorem of Bridge, of course."

"The funda–what?"

"Wait a moment—if you would—" Fumbling inside her carpetbag, Mildred found and extracted a completed needlepoint, then stretched it before Tush's incredulous eyes.

CORKY SCREWS UP

Second to speak, Tush picked up

♠ A K J 7   ♡ A 5 3   ◇ 9 7 5 4 3   ♣ A

and bid 1◇ after Mildred's pass. The auction continued:

West	North	East	South
Harold	*Corky*	*Mildred*	*Tush*
		pass	1◇
pass	1♠	pass	3♣
pass	4♠	all pass	

The ♡Q was led.

Contract: 4♠ by North
Opening lead: ♡Q

Corky
♠ Q 8 4 2
♡ 8 7 2
◇ K 2
♣ K J 7 5

Dummy
♠ A K J 7
♡ A 5 3
◇ 9 7 5 4 3
♣ A

Ducking the first heart, Corky won the continuation, unblocked the
♣A, and came to hand with ♠Q. After ditching dummy's last heart on
the ♣K, she led a trump back to the board (both defenders following)
and a diamond toward her king.

When West rose with the ◇A and continued with the ♡K, Tush saw
Corky's face fall. "I may have blown this," she muttered.

Looking desperate, Corky pitched a diamond from the board instead of ruffing, but it did her no good; Harold continued with the ♣10 (a trump would have been equally good), jack, queen, ruff. Corky could play a diamond to the king and return to the board with a trump to ruff out the suit—it was 3-3—but she couldn't get back to the board to cash the last diamond, and had to lose a club from hand to go down one.

"With the trumps and diamonds splitting, and the ace of diamonds on side, I could have made it," said Corky ruefully. "I got seduced by that heart pitch."

Wondering momentarily what else could seduce her, Tush caught himself and turned to the table display. The full deal had been:

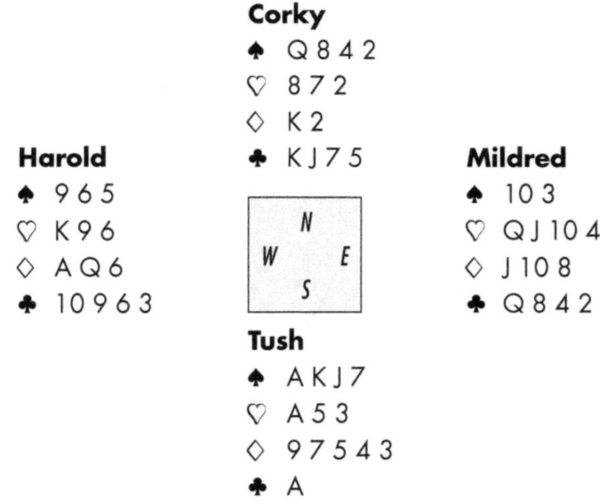

Par was +620 North-South.

"If your king of clubs had been a small card, you'd have made the hand," offered Tush.

"Then I wouldn't have bid game."

Tush laughed. He was secretly pleased that his partner had proved to be fallible, even though they'd have to work hard to get that dozen IMPs back. In any case, a pleasant prospect lay before Tush: dinner and another twenty-six boards. Good company, good bridge, and maybe a nice victory.

TUSH GETS FOOD AND EDIFICATION

Dinner proved to be a buffet of Lebanese food, attractively displayed on a sideboard in a larger, central room. Tush and Corky filled their plates with pita bread and hummus, baba ghanouj, tabbouleh, stuffed grape leaves, and a variety of kibbeh. Looking around for a place to sit, Tush's eye caught two exuberant waves: James and Herbert, with whom they had shared one deal passed out and the other claimed at Trick 1. Indeed, there were empty seats for Tush and Corky at James' and Herbert's table for four.

"What is it," said Tush between two forkfuls of tabbouleh, "with this Ricochet system, that attracts people here? You can't play it outside this club, right? Relay systems are forbidden by the ACBL, and there's other illegal stuff too, I think. Not to mention crypto."

"Before we answer that," replied Herbert, "let me clarify something: crypto's got nothing to do with Ricochet, apart from there being a lot of fans of both here. You can add crypto-conventions to any system, and of course encrypted leads and defensive signals are independent of your bidding system to begin with."

"Okay, then, let's just talk about Ricochet. Why do *you* guys play it?"

"Let me answer that with a question. Have you ever taught bridge to beginners? A lot of folks in this club, regardless of age, are relatively recent converts to bridge. They're really smart people, most of 'em, but they haven't got the time to learn a million special agreements."

"I've never taught bridge at any level. Sounds hard."

"If you tried, you'd soon realize that Standard American is an extremely complex system, with dozens of understandings and special cases that are very hard to codify. The system is one enormous kludge, with understandings piled on top of understandings. It takes years of experience playing tournament bridge to get to the point where you can sit down with a new partner and expect to communicate with any subtlety."

"I'll grant you that, but that's what makes a beginner a beginner, and an expert an expert."

"But does it have to be like that? Shouldn't there be a way for two intelligent amateurs to learn to bid with reasonable effectiveness in, say, weeks instead of months or years?"

"Surely, if they pick the right text, and read it together, they can get up to average 'sectional' level in short order."

"Not without a lot of table time. Think about it. If there were reasonable, consistent rules of bidding, that could be understood without judgment gained from experience, wouldn't it be possible to teach them to a computer?"

"Sure. Lots of computer bridge programs play Standard American."

"But they're terrible! Wouldn't you think that, with all the money and effort that goes into commercial software production, these programs would be expert bidders? They're just awful! Do you read 'It's Your Call' in the *ACBL Bulletin*? They use a computer program, one of the better ones, as a panelist. But its choices are frequently bad and sometimes downright pathetic."

"Be that as it may, you have to remember that Standard American was developed to be used by people, not computers."

"I'm not so sure," Corky put in. "If we actually designed systems for people, real people, there'd be some conventions for the imperfect. I've heard of a few. 'Audit Blackwood,' for example: four clubs Gerber, followed by four notrump, asking partner to count aces again and make sure. Or the Four Diamond Convention, which is used to say 'I take back my last bid,' and demands that partner ask for a review."

"Corky makes a good point," Herbert continued. "Standard American is hard for computers *and* people. But a good system shouldn't be hard for computers. You're asking a computer to make one of a very limited number of choices, based on combinatorial information. Computers do that kind of thing very well, if they have a reasonable set of rules to follow. I'm not talking about asking the computer to understand psychology, read the opponents' faces, use gamesmanship, or play like Zia. Just make good, sensible bids."

"Hey," pursued Tush, "bridge is a tough game. And the problems they give to expert bidding panels are designed to be difficult. The human experts disagree all the time. In *The Bridge World*'s Master Solvers' Club, they relish problems where they can get votes for every non-jump call. Anyway, what has this got to do with Ricochet? Are you going to tell me that in every situation there's a clear-cut call? If so, I'm not going to believe you."

"Heavens, no. No system of any value can have that property. The idea of Ricochet is that decisions are made by certain principles, instead of on a case-by-case basis. That way, two smart people, or two computers, for that matter, can quickly arrive at *some* way to communicate, without having to consider a million different auctions. Then, they can gradually refine it to make it more efficient."

"It used to be thought that when paired with each other, computers could bid without principles," said Herbert. "The idea was, they could consider every possible continuation, and optimize. But that never happened—it's just not possible for a computer to think that far ahead, except near the end of an auction. Combinatorial explosion. Try asking a computer what an opening bid of one heart should show. Hopeless! You can get computers to 'play it by ear,' so to speak, and invent as they bid. But not without principles."

"Are you telling me there are no principles in standard bidding? How about 'fast arrival'? Or 'highest of touching suits'? Or Rubens' 'Useful-Space'? Or 'pass then pull invites'? Or 'double behind for penalties, before for takeout?' Or—"

"Sure, sure, but most of these either have very limited application, or they're not in general use, or both. You don't teach with 'em, except maybe 'new suit forcing.' You teach by saying here's what you need to open, here's what you need to respond, here's the weakest suit you can bid in this situation, here's what you need in some other situation. Here's what an overcall means, here's a list of forcing bids, here's a list of takeout doubles, optional doubles and penalty doubles… and of course these lists are never complete. Half the partnerships playing bridge haven't even decided whether new suit response to an overcall is forcing. You and Corky are playing Yellow Card, right? It takes pages even to write out that simplified version of Standard. But suppose Corky opens one club and reverses to two diamonds after your heart response, and you hold something like

♠ x x x x   ♡ K Q x x   ♢ Q x x   ♣ x x

What are you expected to bid? The system doesn't tell you. And it's basic!"

"Give me a break," said Tush. "Corky and I just met. If we'd had time to go over our system, we'd have agreed on how to keep the bidding alive after a reverse. Some pairs would bid two spades with that hand, for example."

"Ricochet players bid two spades, too," James interjected. "But they don't need to have discussed it. It comes from the 'neutral response' principle."

"We've seen that in operation," said Corky. "Anytime you are obliged to keep the bidding open, you have some call available which says 'I have nothing particular I want to show.' "

"The idea of this principle," Herbert resumed, "is to generalize a principle that everyone recognizes: 'pass' says 'nothing to show.' Very useful when the opponents have bid in front of you. But they don't always do you that favor; then, you may have nothing to show, but can't pass. Having a neutral bid is incredibly useful: after takeout doubles, negative doubles, reverses, forcing passes, big openers, big responses…"

"Just the other day," said James, "I read an expert pointing out that after one club, double, bidding one diamond can be a big help to the opposition. Why? Because, now, a non-jump bid by your left-hand opponent actually means something. If you pass and lefty bids one heart, righty has to allow that he might have three hearts and a bust. If you bid, lefty can pass whenever he has nothing to say, and that is a huge boon to the opponents' communication."

"Against Ricochet opponents," Herbert explained, "it wouldn't matter, because after one club, double, pass, a call of one diamond is neutral—the same as a pass would be after one club, double, one diamond."

"Not to belabor the obvious," countered Tush, "you can't then use one diamond naturally."

"Big deal. If you really have diamonds, bid two."

"And if it's one heart that partner doubled, are you saying I can no longer respond one spade naturally?"

"Right. But you'll never buy it for one spade, anyway. And partner can't compete further in spades without a mountain, since you might have a bust."

"And if it's *two* hearts that she doubled? Are you saying we can't get to two spades?"

"Ah. Two spades is a twobelow. If she doubles two hearts, two spades is to play. Your neutral bid is two notrump."

"Um, a tubelo?"

"Two below game. Normally the neutral call is the cheapest bid, but if that bid is a logical contract which happens to be a slam, a game, or two tricks below game, it is natural and you have to go higher to get to the neutral call. Like in the reverse situation we talked about before: after one club, pass, one heart, pass, two diamonds, pass, 'two hearts' is natural so 'two spades' is neutral."

"Hmm," said Tush. "So, the twobelows are two of a major, three of a minor, or one notrump?"

"Exactly. We have to give up stopping one trick below game sometimes. There are exceptions in competition, for more advanced Ricocheters."

"Seems like over a weak two-bid, Ricocheters are playing Lebensohl."

"Not really. It's not a relay to three clubs for us. But the point is, we don't have to discuss it in advance."

"Actually," contributed James, "there are a surprising number of places where Ricochet does accidentally agree with standard. For example, two diamonds in response to Stayman is a classic Ricochet neutral."

"Nothing accidental about it," said Herbert. "Neutral bids are necessary, so Standard American has them, but on a case-by-case basis. If you open a major and rebid it in Standard American, it's supposed to show six. But if you open one heart and partner bids two diamonds, which of course is forcing in standard, the agreement is that two hearts is neutral—it doesn't really even *suggest* extra length. You have to have a neutral bid, and that's the one chosen."

"You see neutral bids more and more," said James. "Part of the reason, I think, is that the opponents interfere all the time now, so people get used to having that nice 'pass' available when they have nothing to show. A neutral two diamonds, after an artificial strong two club opener, has been standard since the beginning of weak two-bids. But now, lots of folks use double negatives as well. In Ricochet, of course, you get as many negatives as you want, for free."

Tush bit into a stuffed grape leaf and pondered. "I can see some problems with this neutral bid principle," he said, still chewing. "For example, teaching a beginner—or worse, a computer—when a twobelow is a 'logical contract.' But, there must be more principles, right? You can't build a system out of bids that say nothing."

"Oh, of course," said James. "For example, like other relay systems, we have a captaincy principle: unlimited hands have artificial forcing bids available, with which they can take control, listen to partner's description, and set the contract. Obvious examples: our opening forcing club, and even more important in Ricochet, our forcing one notrump response (and two diamonds over our natural two club opener)."

"But in Ricochet," continued Herbert, "there's always one neutral response and the rest are natural. This makes it easy to learn and much easier to recover from errors."

"Not to quibble," said Tush, "but is it obvious what 'natural' means when you haven't already got an understanding about standard bidding?"

"You're right. You still need to teach basic ideas like bidding long suits first, showing your strength and stoppers, planning ahead, and so forth. That's a good thing, I think, because these ideas pervade all systems that a beginner is likely to see at the bridge table. Plus, most of the time Ricochet players are not relaying—at least, they shouldn't be. Then their bidding is not so far from standard. So they need to learn basic bridge sense."

"For example," said James, "a Ricochet beginner learns to bid two clubs neutral on

♠ K Q x x x ♡ A x ♢ x x ♣ K x x x

after partner has responded one notrump to his or her one spade opener, because three clubs is too high for that suit. Whereas, with the minors reversed, its an automatic two diamond call."

"There are more principles, too," said Herbert, "for example, you jump with fits, stay low with misfits, cuebid first-round controls first. But, number one, you still need special agreements for certain situations; principles don't cover everything. And number two, very important, you willingly give up optimality for consistency. Ricochet doesn't even try to be perfect."

"One thing Ricochet does try to do," said James, "is to give most calls the same meaning regardless of interference. For example, beginners hate it when you teach them responses to an opening bid, then tell them it's all different if right-hand opponent doubles, or overcalls, or if you're a passed hand. Are these situations really so different? The opponents will often get in the auction regardless, so you should always expect competition. In standard, one heart - pass - three hearts is limited but one heart - double - three hearts is preemptive. Absurd!

The preemptive jump raise is more effective, not less, if they haven't got a double in."

"What James is saying," offered Herbert, "is that a system that gives up being perfect can be much simpler, at little cost."

"When I was in college," said James, "some guys wrote up a system called M-Z-M whose mantra was 'a bid for every hand, a hand for every bid.' I loved the idea at the time, but as with most things, I have lowered expectations in my old age!"

Corky, who had been listening while feasting, raised a finger. "Really, all systems are made up of principles and special agreements, wouldn't you say? With lots of compromises. Is Ricochet really so different from, say, Precision?"

"Maybe not qualitatively," replied Herbert. "But quantitatively, many fewer special agreements are required. You know, people forget that there are a zillion different things that can happen in an auction. You can't keep more than a few in your brain at one time. If you actually try to think of all the different kinds of bidding problems there are, and all the special agreements you'd need to handle them if you didn't have principles, it would boggle your mind."

"Actually," said James, "there are many more possible auctions than deals. Most people don't realize that."

Tush put on a skeptical face. "Surely you jest. The number of deals is astronomical, some fifty-digit number, no? You never see the same deal twice, even if you ignore spot cards. Whereas, the bidding goes one notrump, pass, three notrump, pass, pass, pass, three times a session."

"Yes, but *critical* auctions—those that take place when lots of IMPs hang on the final contract—are often unique. It's hard to keep that in mind because deals appear uniformly at random, auctions don't. Mathematically speaking, most auctions end in seven notrump and take about thirty rounds to get there; these don't occur in real life. But, if you're not convinced there are more auctions than deals, I can show you a bidding system that will produce a different auction for every deal."

"Hard to imagine how that would work," said Tush dubiously.

"Actually, it's simple in principle. Of course, it's a cooperative system, not designed to reach a good contract, only to reveal your hand. Here's a toy version: list all the cards in some order, say, ace of spades, ace of hearts, ace of diamonds, ace of clubs, king of spades, et cetera. The cards are located in that order. Whenever it's your turn to bid, you pass unless you have the card in question. If you do have it, you make the lowest bid, unless you also have the *next* card in question, in which case you skip that bid."

"Hmm," mused Tush. "So the person with the ace of spades opens the bidding with one club? Or higher, if he also has the ace of hearts. The auction won't die with four passes, because *somebody* has to have the next card."

Corky was doing some calculating. "Won't this run out too soon? There are fifty-two cards, but only—let's see—five times seven equals thirty-five bids."

"Yes," said James, "it does run out, but we haven't used doubles. With doubles and redoubles, there are twenty-two ways to get from, say, three hearts to three spades, instead of only four. With a little work, you can use the added flexibility to locate *two* cards for every bid."

A few seconds of silence passed.

"Not the most practical of systems," Corky offered.

"But note, since there are twenty-six pairs of cards to consider, all the auctions end at six diamonds. This is handy, because—"

"Let me guess," said Tush, mopping up his last bit of hummus. "Because six diamonds always makes."

TUSH GETS HORNSWOGGLED

Feeling full but happy, Tush followed Corky back to Table 7, finding their old friends George and Tricia already seated. After a few favorable words about the food, and two passes, Tush contemplated a nice hand:

♠K 10 9 3 2   ♡A K 4   ◇A K 7   ♣4 3

Too nice, perhaps, to open 1NT; four and a half quick tricks and a five-card major. So Tush began with 1♠, and then immediately second-guessed himself. Partner would respond 1NT, no doubt, which he would raise to two; and Corky would end up playing 2NT or 3NT with all Tush's lovely aces and kings sunbathing on the table. Tush hadn't forgotten his own experience playing 3NT upside down.

The big club players could rebid 1NT over a negative response, and maybe play it there, or get raised and declare three from the right side. Or would they rebid 1♠?

While this speculation was going on in Tush's head, the other players were entering their calls, and it was the opponents who had reached 3NT.

West	North	East	South
Tricia	*Corky*	*George*	*Tush*
	pass	pass	1♠
1NT	pass	2NT	pass
3NT	all pass		

Corky led the ♣6 and the dummy was spread.

Contract: 3NT by West
Opening lead: ♠6

Dummy
♠ 8 5
♡ J 10 2
◇ J 10 3
♣ Q J 10 9 8

Tush
♠ K 10 9 3 2
♡ A K 4
◇ A K 7
♣ 4 3

East was apologetic. "I figured, with all these spots, and all the opponents' strength in one hand..." Tricia waved off his explanation and called for a low spade from dummy. Tush inserted the nine, won by declarer's queen.

Well, thought Tush, at least I got my spade lead—but did I want one? Tush was under no illusions about the location of the ♠J; declarer no doubt had that card along with every other missing honor. Tush counted declarer's tricks: five in clubs, at least three in spades, and whatever could be set up in the red suits. This is a cold game, thought Tush, and everyone else sitting South would be defending a partial. Shoot!

Declarer cashed ace-king of clubs, Corky echoing seven-deuce, but then Tricia paused; the next card out of her hand was the ♡Q.

Tush perked up. The clubs were blocked! Could he keep declarer off the board? Not if he won this trick, that was for sure. He ducked smartly, and when declarer tried the ◇Q, he ducked again.

It was not hard to foresee the outcome. Tush would be thrown in with his red-suit winners, but would be careful to exit with a high spade, leaving declarer in her hand. Then he would sit back and wait to take the setting trick with his remaining spade honor.

What happened next was confusing to Tush; declarer seemed to have led a club from her hand. Surely, that card had already been played, or was it from another deck? No, it was Corky who showed out, as dummy won the queen and followed with two more good clubs.

The full deal had been:

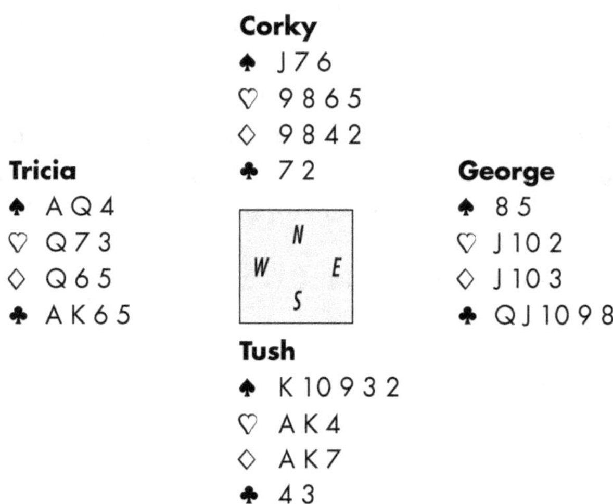

Tush, in a fog, pitched a spade on the ♣Q but seemed to have nothing to spare on dummy's last two club winners. He and the board had come down to:

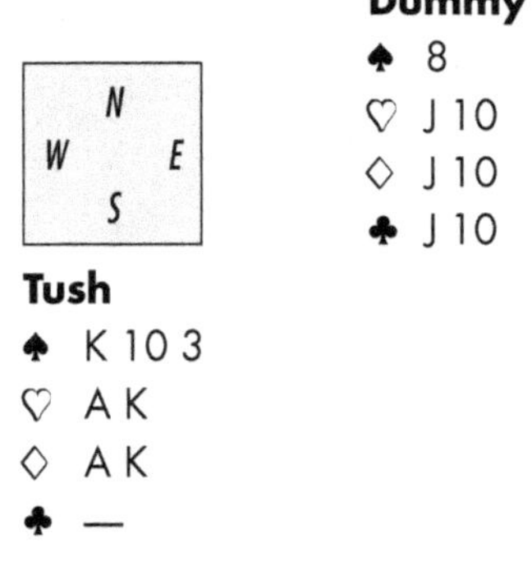

Still thinking (or, perhaps desperately hoping) that declarer had started with four or five spades to the ♠AQJ, he pitched his red kings. Tricia then exited a heart and claimed an overtrick.

"Too bad we're not playing Smith echo," said Tush to Corky, trying not to look mortified. But there was no gainsaying the fact that he had let a hopeless game come home, not to mention blowing three opportunities to win his four top tricks in the red suits.

Corky sighed as she entered their −430 against par (+110 to East-West for a club partial), -8 IMPs. "You couldn't at least have saved an IMP at the end? You really thought she was 5-2-2-4?"

Tricia maintained her bland, pleasant expression, not looking at all like someone who had just brought off a brilliant 12-IMP swindle. George, however, who had not really followed the play, could not be stifled. "Those spots really come in handy, don't they?" he babbled. "I'm telling you, my hand was worth *much* more than five points, more like eight. They should count a half point for each ten, a quarter for each nine..."

"Anyone have a Tylenol?" asked Corky.

TUSH MISSES THE POINT

Tush pulled himself together. West had made a nice play, but so what? It would not have worked against a lesser defender than Tush. Time to get back in the game.

George, on Tush's right, began with a 3◇ preempt. Red against white with

♠ A Q J 8 6 5   ♡ 5   ◇ 8 7 4   ♣ K Q 6

Tush overcalled 3♠.

This was followed by pass, 4NT, pass back to Tush. Yipes—did Yellow Card have Keycard Blackwood? Surely not, thought Tush, but luckily he didn't need to know. Five diamonds was his call either way.

But now the bidding took an unexpected turn: double, pass, pass, back to Tush!

West	North	East	South
Tricia	*Corky*	*George*	*Tush*
		3◇	3♠
pass	4NT	pass	5◇
dbl	pass	pass	?

What now? What in heaven's name did Corky want from him? She must have had some follow-up in mind after she asked for aces; she certainly can't have been planning to drop him in five of the opponents' suit. Was she worried about a diamond control? That made no sense, she could have raised 3♠ to five. Heart control? Club control? She'd have started cuebidding instead of asking for aces. Trump king? Extra strength?

Well, if it was one of the latter two, Tush didn't have it. He bid 5♠.

Pass, *five* notrump, pass.

Ugh. Was this just a Blackwood continuation, or could she actually be trying to play the hand in 5NT? If the former, and Tush passed, it could be a major disaster. Bidding on was safer. Plus, Tush was trying hard to be a reliable partner and not overthink. So he bid 6♢, showing his one king.

Moments later, Corky was in 6NT doubled, and George was agonizing over his lead.

West	North	East	South
Tricia	*Corky*	*George*	*Tush*
		3♢	3♠
pass	4NT	pass	5♢
dbl	pass	pass	5♠
pass	5NT	pass	6♢
pass	6NT	pass	pass
dbl	all pass		

Finally, the ♣7 hit the table, and Tush put down his dummy.

Contract: 6NT doubled,
       by North
Opening lead: ♣7

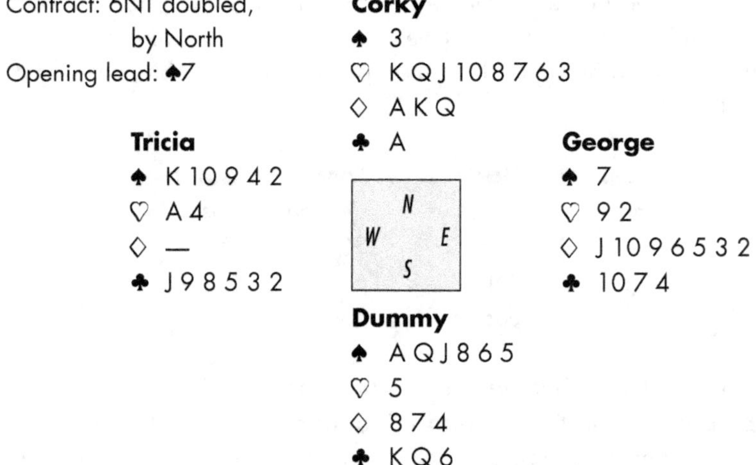

Corky
♠ 3
♡ K Q J 10 8 7 6 3
♢ A K Q
♣ A

Tricia
♠ K 10 9 4 2
♡ A 4
♢ —
♣ J 9 8 5 3 2

George
♠ 7
♡ 9 2
♢ J 10 9 6 5 3 2
♣ 10 7 4

Dummy
♠ A Q J 8 6 5
♡ 5
♢ 8 7 4
♣ K Q 6

Corky, looking unhappy, played the ace and continued with a heart from the table. Tricia went up with the ace and cashed the ♠K; Corky claimed the rest, for down one.

Even after the deal appeared on the table it took Tush a minute to comprehend what had happened. Tricia, with her spade stack, had suspected that Corky was aiming for a heart slam; her double of five diamonds was for the lead. "Oh my god," Tush said to Corky. "You were trying to get me to bid the hearts, so the diamond void would be on lead. I should have figured it out—all those hearts had to be somewhere!"

"Don't fret about it," said Corky. "I was really reaching. I probably should've just bid five hearts over the double and settled for game."

"Nonsense—I could easily have had both black kings. Then you could pass my six heart response to Blackwood. Or bid a cold six notrump, for that matter. Anyway, the actual contract wasn't that bad—George here might not have had a spade to lead."

"Or he might not have led his spade," said George himself. "I had some difficulty with this auction as well."

In any case, that was a loss of 17 IMPs for Tush and Corky against +1440 for 6NT by *South*. "Tough par," said Tricia sympathetically.

Tush was despondent. Time after time, Corky had come through for him, and now when it was his turn, he had let her down. If he could only rewind the tape, and bid the hearts: was that too much to ask?

TUSH PLAYS THE WRONG CARD

Tush looked up to find that George and Tricia had been replaced by the portly gentlemen from Round 2. This time, Tush took the initiative and introduced himself.

"My name's Robert, too," said West.

"Mine's Aloysius," said East, between swigs of a 24-ounce diet cola, "but people call me Ace."

Tush picked up his hand. With

♠ K Q 9   ♡ 4   ◇ A K J 6 4   ♣ 10 9 8 5

he had a 1◇ opener, as dealer, but then the opponents quickly took over.

West	North	East	South
Robert	Corky	Ace	Tush
			1◇
dbl	2◇	3◇	pass
3♠	pass	3NT	pass
4♡	pass	4♠	all pass

Corky led the ◇8.

Contract: 4♠ by West
Opening lead: ◊8

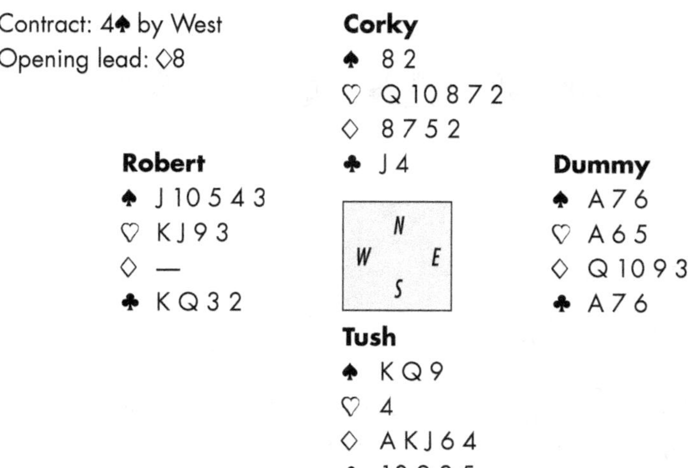

Corky
♠ 8 2
♡ Q 10 8 7 2
◊ 8 7 5 2
♣ J 4

Robert
♠ J 10 5 4 3
♡ K J 9 3
◊ —
♣ K Q 3 2

Dummy
♠ A 7 6
♡ A 6 5
◊ Q 10 9 3
♣ A 7 6

Tush
♠ K Q 9
♡ 4
◊ A K J 6 4
♣ 10 9 8 5

Declarer played the ◊9 from dummy and ruffed Tush's ◊J. A club to the ♣A was followed by a low trump from the board, won by Tush's ♠Q.

Tush exited with the ♣10, won by declarer with the ♣Q. There followed a trump to the ace, a club back to the king, and a club ruffed on the board.

Declarer took some time, then led the ◊Q from the board, covered and ruffed. Next came a heart to the table and a small heart through Tush. Naturally Tush declined to ruff this, but West won the king and put Tush in with his high trump.

Tush cashed his high diamond but dummy's ◊10 took the game-going trick, matching par exactly.

"Nicely played," said Tush to West. "I don't think I can do anything to stop it."

"Thanks. If you win that first trump lead with the king, though, I'm going down."

Tush gave him a stare. "I did win it, didn't I?"

"Not with the king. You won it with the queen."

"Um, aren't they equals?"

"Not in this case. The thing is, I have an alternative line: give up on the club ruff, and finesse the trumps through your partner instead. That's what I planned if you had won trick three with the king. But you wouldn't be hopping up with the queen from Qx , so I abandoned the finesse."

Tush saw the point, but was not a gracious loser. "Next time, no doubt, it'll be my *partner* who needs to divine the trump suit, and I'll regret playing the king."

TUSH PLAYS TOO FAST

Tush looked up from

$$\spadesuit 5 \quad \heartsuit A54 \quad \diamondsuit Q873 \quad \clubsuit K9842$$

to see his right-hand opponent, Ace, take another long swig of his diet cola. West gave his partner a withering glance. "Keep guzzling that stuff, and you know what's going to happen," he said sternly. Tush could only guess what West was alluding to. Kidney problems? Brain damage?

The auction began with two passes and a 2◊ opener by the soft drink. The table told Tush that this was no ordinary weak two-bid:

```
11-15 HCP, 3-SUITER SHORT IN ◊
DEFAULT DEFENSE: DBL = DIAMOND SUIT
2NT = 16-19 BALANCED
```

Tush waited for the display to allow him to make his call, then passed.

West, the other Robert, responded with a natural, invitational 2NT, and was raised to three.

West	North	East	South
Robert	Corky	Ace	Tush
pass	pass	2◊	pass
2NT	pass	3NT	all pass

Great, thought Tush. We get to defend another 3NT with only a vague idea of the declarer's hand. At least Corky gets to lead, this time.

Her opening shot was the ♠6; dummy came down with about what Tush expected.

Contract: 3NT by West
Opening lead: ♣6

Dummy
♠ A J 7 4
♡ K Q J 10
♢ J
♣ Q 7 6 3

Tush
♠ 5
♡ A 5 4
♢ Q 8 7 3
♣ K 9 8 4 2

West contemplated dummy, in perfect quiet, while Tush readied himself to extract his lone spade. Suddenly a thundering burp from East ripped through the air. "Ace!" screamed West, and Tush tossed his five on the table.

Silence again reigned for a few seconds, as everyone absorbed what had just happened. Then Corky, shaking her head, pushed her DIRECTOR button.

P-G was on the scene almost instantly. "I led a spade against three notrump," Corky explained. "Declarer appeared to call for the ace, but was actually just yelling at dummy. Before this could be clarified, my partner followed to the trick."

"You called out 'Ace' ?" P-G asked of West. "When it was dummy's turn to play?"

"I was provoked," said West. "It was not intentional."

Running his hand through his inch-long white hair, P-G circumnavigated the table, studying the hands, then paused. "Robert, what card did you intend to play?"

"What do you mean?" Tush replied. "I only have one—oh, shit." Too late, Tush realized the question had not been directed at him.

"My partner's name is Robert also," said Corky.

P-G blinked. "What is this, 'Who's-on-first Day' ?"

"Sorry, P-G. It's my fault," said East. Sighing, P-G turned to Tush. "You, Robert, Mr. South. Pick whatever spade you would like for dummy's play." Tush tilted his head left, then right.

"Um, I guess, the ace, then."

"Okay, let play resume. Corky, please call me back if you think there might have been any damage to your side." With that pronouncement, P-G trudged off.

West reached across to play dummy's ♠A, and Tush pointed to his five, still on the table. The cards were turned, and West now called for the ♡K.

Tush pounced on this with his ace. A diamond shift was called for, clearly, and the proper card to lead was the queen, smothering dummy's jack. At least, he should get a decent board out of this, for a change.

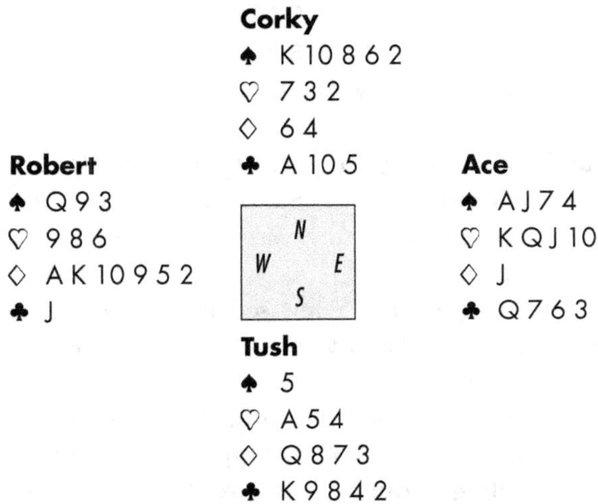

Six diamonds, three hearts and the beleaguered ♠A made for +630 to East and West, 10 IMPs against their +140 par for a spade partial.

Corky slid her cards back in, with a miffed look at Tush. "You could at least have held up your ace for a round or two, looking for a signal."

Tush thought fast. "That would have put you in an ethical bind, right? Since everyone knows I had no spade to lead back, your signals would be unfairly unambiguous for the minors."

"Hey," said West. "You two really did get shortchanged. I think we should get P-G back."

"No!" cried Tush. "I mean, thank you for the offer, but we—or I, anyway—earned the result." All I need, thought Tush, is for my play to be examined by the director.

"Well, good luck, then," said West as he and his partner got up. They were clear out of the room—visually, at least—when the rumble of another burp reached Tush's ears.

TUSH GETS AN ENCRYPTED LEAD

Dan and Daniella had returned to Table 7, this time with Daniella in the East chair. Holding

♠ A K Q 4   ♡ K 6   ◇ Q 9 3   ♣ 10 9 8 5

after two passes, Tush opened a shaded 1NT. A Stayman sequence left him in 3NT. I'd better make it, he thought grimly.

West	North	East	South
Dan	Corky	Daniella	Tush
	pass	pass	1NT
pass	2♣	pass	2♠
pass	3NT	all pass	

The ◇5 was led, and dummy spread.

Contract: 3NT by South
Opening lead: ◇5

Dummy
♠ 8 3
♡ A Q 5 4
◇ 8 6 2
♣ A Q 3 2

Tush
♠ A K Q 4
♡ K 6
◇ Q 9 3
♣ 10 9 8 5

The table flashed in front of Tush:

```
ENCRYPTED LEAD
EVEN NUMBER OF SPADES » EVEN LEADS
ODD » ODD
```

Tush turned to his right-hand opponent. "Can you explain this? What's a diamond lead got to do with spades?"

"When you showed four spades in the bidding," Daniella replied, "it set up a key for encrypting the opening lead. When the dummy is put down, I can count how many spades my partner has, and interpret his lead correctly; you can't.

"The way we do it is that partner leads ordinary fourth-best if he has an even number of spades, but uses third-fifth opening leads otherwise. Even even, odd odd. Easy to remember. Actually, we also base the rest of the signaling for that deal on the same key; upside-down in the odd case."

Tush stopped to consider. "What if I have five spades?"

"Then I might misread the lead, but I also might read it correctly and make a useful deduction about your spade length."

"Even worse, what if I can work out from the circumstances which kind of lead your partner made, and then use it to play the spades correctly?"

"That could happen—in fact, that's why some cryppie fans don't like suit-length key. But we find that in most cases, by the time declarer figures out whether the opening lead was even or odd, the die is cast on the fate of the hand."

Tush sighed and turned his attention back to the deal, playing a small diamond from the board. East won the ace and continued with the ◇J.

Let's see, thought Tush. Three tricks in each major, three more in clubs unless the king and jack are both with East. The big problem is to avoid losing four diamond tricks, along with the club. Well, if East had been dealt ace, jack and a small card in diamonds, Tush's play was immaterial, so forget that. If East had ◇AJ doubleton, Tush could simply duck the jack. On the other hand, if East began with ◇AJ10, Tush needed to rise with the queen to block the suit. Which to play for?

Either way, West had led his second-smallest diamond; either fourth-best from ♢K10754, or third-best from ♢K754. Putting all his information together, Tush deduced that if West had an odd number of spades, the ♢J should be ducked; if an even number, it should be covered.

Why not play the spades and find out? Duh, because the decision has to be made now, not later.

This is stupid. Does restricted choice apply? No, because with ♢AJ10 East cannot lead back the ten; that would force declarer to cover as his only chance.

There must be some clue. Well, there was restricted choice of a sort: West, with only four diamonds to the king, *might* have led some other suit. Five to the king-ten, on the other hand, was an irresistible suit to lead from against 3NT.

And, one other point: if Tush ducked and East did have the ten, the opponents could only run four diamonds. Tush might still recover by finding both club honors on-side.

So Tush ducked, but the hands were not what he had hoped for.

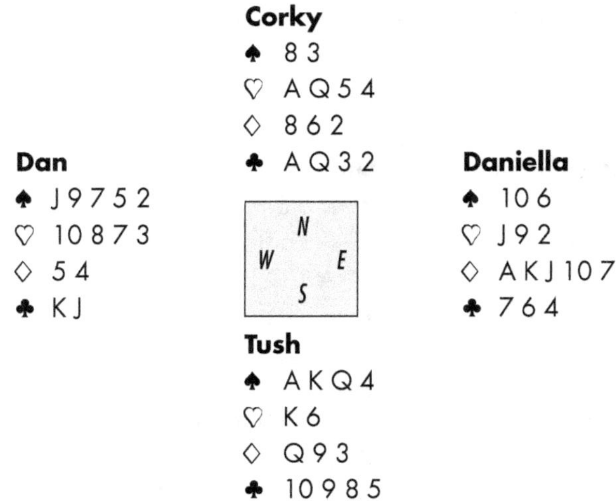

So that was down one for Tush, yet another 13-IMP loss against the +660 par. This was not good. He and Corky needed to get back on the rails, if they were going to have any chance to win.

TUSH ENCOUNTERS A CRYPTO-FALSECARD

Holding

♠ A 10 9 8 7 4 ♥ 8 ♦ 10 7 5 ♣ K J 6

Tush opened 2♠ second in hand; the rest of the auction was out of his control.

West	North	East	South
Dan	*Corky*	*Daniella*	*Tush*
		pass	2♠
pass	4NT	pass	5♦
pass	6♠	all pass	

The ♥2 was led.

Contract: 6♠ by South
Opening lead: ♥2

Dummy
♠ K 6 3
♥ A J 6 3
♦ A K Q J 3
♣ 4

Tush
♠ A 10 9 8 7 4
♥ 8
♦ 10 7 5
♣ K J 6

The table flashed once more in front of Tush, with a familiar message:

Tush turned once more to his right-hand opponent, Daniella. "You do this *anytime* declarer reveals his precise length in some suit? I mean, against notrump, I understand, but you're playing with fire here. Plus, declarer is likely to find out soon enough how the trumps are distributed, and then he can read your lead."

"True," East admitted. "But then we're no worse off than the non-encrypted leaders. And to the extent that trumps aren't drawn immediately, we get our signals encrypted for free."

"Plus," West chimed in, "the deal isn't always played in the suit whose length was revealed."

Tush didn't buy this, and moreover, he was beginning to think he could turn the convention on its head on this very deal. Clearly, he needed to pick up the trumps; might it not help if he could divine the lead-type?

Winning the ♡A on the board, he ruffed a heart in hand and then led the ten of trumps, covered by the jack and king. Rather than finessing against East's presumed queen, thus staking everything on restricted choice, Tush ruffed a second heart in hand.

Seeing that he might want two more entries to the board, Tush exited with a club from hand and won the diamond return in dummy. Finally, he ruffed out the last heart—to which both East and West followed.

Aha! Hearts had been 4-4, thus the lead was fourth best, thus West had an even number of trumps! Sweet triumph. Tush plunked down the ♠A and pumped a fist as the queen fell on his left.

Oops, wait, was that the queen of *clubs*? Tush recoiled in horror. East followed suit, then held up her ♠Q to claim down one. The hands had been:

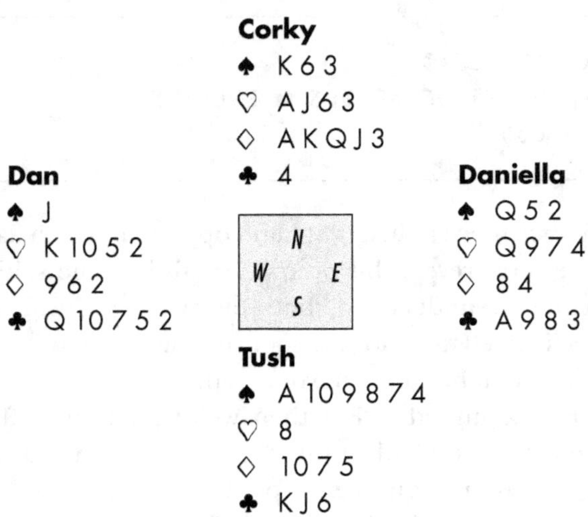

"I thought it might be dangerous to lead honestly, holding the stiff jack of trumps," Dan explained.

Corky sighed and shook her head, entering –50 against the par of +990 for 6NT by South. Another 14 IMPs away. Tush closed his eyes and let out a breath. Things were definitely not going well.

TUSH SUCCUMBS TO A THIRD-ORDER THROW-IN

Tush shaded his eyes as Loud Sweater and his partner approached the table and seated themselves, with a brief but friendly greeting from each. Holding

♠J 10 9 7 ♡A 10 9 8 ♢QJ 6 ♣QJ

Tush witnessed the following remarkable Ricochet auction:

West	North	East	South
			pass
1♣	pass	1♢	pass
1♡	pass	1♠	pass
2♣	pass	2♢	pass
2♡	pass	2♠	pass
2NT	pass	3♣	pass
3NT	all pass		

Every bid of West's except the final 3NT had been described as

FORCING, WAITING

Every bid of East's was

NEUTRAL, NOTHING TO SHOW

The initial 1◇ response was further described

`NEGATIVE, FEWER THAN 9 HCP`

"It seems that you two have taken six rounds of bidding to show absolutely zilch," said Tush.

"In a sense, yes," agreed West, the young woman. "But that says a lot. My partner's one diamond showed either a weak hand or no good suit; one spade, a very weak hand. Over two clubs, he'd have bid any half-decent major suit, since he could do so cheaply, or maybe two notrump with a couple of quacks. Likewise, over my two hearts, he'd have bid any sort of minor, or two notrump with even one quack. Finally, over my two notrump he had room to mention even four babies in any suit other than clubs. So, he's pretty much forced to have a flat bust with four clubs. "Of course, we've never had anywhere near that many neutrals before, so all this is really guesswork based on Ricochet principles. Hopefully, my partner's on the same wavelength—?"

East laughed. "One of those principles being that with natural relays, a minor misunderstanding shouldn't cause a major disaster!"

"And what," pursued Tush, "did opener show?"

"Since she relayed at every turn—skipping one notrump on the third round, which would have shown 19-21 balanced—she obviously has a mountain. Probably looking in vain for a four-four fit. Thinks she can make three notrump with no help. Good luck, partner."

Corky looked up, her eyes asking if Tush was through. He shrugged and gave a come-on signal; Corky put the ♣5 on the table. East put his dummy down with pride. "Extra nine for you, partner."

Contract: 3NT by West
Opening lead: ♣5

Dummy
♠ 6 3 2
♡ 6 5 3
◇ 8 5 4
♣ 9 8 6 3

Tush
♠ J 10 9 7
♡ A 10 9 8
◇ Q J 6
♣ Q J

The opening club lead went to Tush's jack and declarer's ace. After some thought, declarer exited a club to Corky's four and Tush's queen. Now what? Obviously declarer had nearly all the remaining high cards, and he and Corky had no chance to set up and run clubs. Notwithstanding, it seemed that Tush might be able to scrape up four more tricks for the defense. With just a smidgen of optimism, he led the ♠J.

Declarer won the queen, and played the ♡K. Tush won and continued hearts, but to no avail; after West cashed the ♡Q and ♡J, he found himself back in with the fourth round of hearts.

Now, if Tush exited another high spade, declarer would win and throw Tush back in with the third round of diamonds, collecting her ninth trick in spades on the endplay. Instead Tush tried getting out with a high diamond, but declarer cashed her remaining two spade tops and threw Tush in with a spade, earning her ninth trick in diamonds.

The full deal:

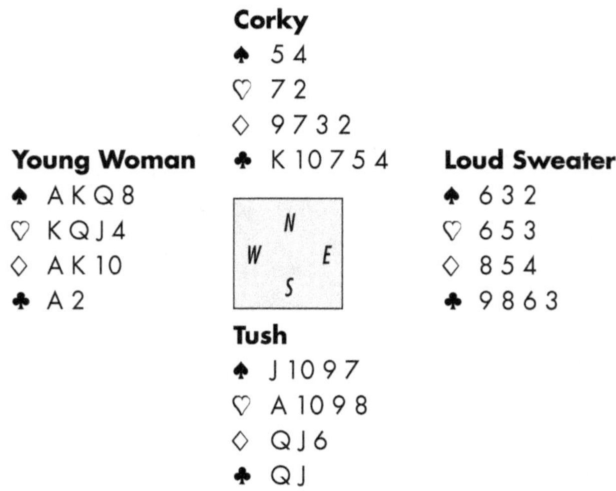

"Nothing we could do," said Corky. "Double-dummy, she's always cold. If you exit a red suit at Trick 3, she puts you in with the fourth round of spades, then later gets an endplay in the red suits one way or the other. You were endplayed at Trick 3."

"Wait a minute, I didn't give up a trick until the third time I got in."

"Yes, but you were forced to set up that last endplay the second time you got in, and you were forced to set up *that* endplay the first time you got in."

Tush felt dizzy. First non-material squeezes, then non-material endplays? Worse, endplays whose effect was to set up other non-material endplays? Wait. "What if you go up with the king of clubs at Trick 2, then continue with the ten?"

"Oh, really? And what do you propose to discard? No, our only chance is if you lead your seven of spades at Trick 3. Not an obvious play, I admit."

At least we didn't lose any IMPs, thought Tush. Small consolation.

TUSH IS SEDUCED BY A FALLACY

Last to speak, Tush watched as West opened with a forcing club and East responded 2♡, NATURAL AND POSITIVE. Further inquiry established that a *one* heart response would have shown a balanced positive, with three or fewer controls (a king being one control, an ace two). 2♡ showed 9 HCP and a decent heart suit of five or more cards, forcing to game; the auction would continue with relays by West until she chose to break the chain.

Holding

♠A Q J 9 8   ♡Q 9 5 4   ◇6   ♣A 9 3

Tush typed in 2♠ and was somewhat surprised to see

WEST	NORTH	EAST	SOUTH
1♣	PASS	2♡	2♠
DBL	PASS	PASS	

appear on his table screen. Tush passed, of course, but not unhappily: had he found a brilliant two-level sacrifice against a game?

West	North	East	South
1♣	pass	2♡	2♠
dbl	all pass		

The ♡3 was led and Corky put down her hand.

Contract: 2♠ doubled, by South
Opening lead: ♡3

Dummy
- ♠ 10 4
- ♡ J 6
- ◊ 8 7 5 2
- ♣ Q 10 7 5 4

Tush
- ♠ A Q J 9 8
- ♡ Q 9 5 4
- ◊ 6
- ♣ A 9 3

East won the ♡K and shot back a trump to the nine and king. West continued a small trump on which East pitched the ◊J, and Tush allowed the board's ten to hold the trick. Now what?

It must be right to play on clubs, thought Tush, and considering her opening bid, West ought to have the king. Accordingly, Tush played a club to his ace and continued with a small one out of hand, won by West's king as East followed twice.

West paused, then switched to a diamond, won by East's ten. East cashed the ♡A, her partner throwing the defense's last club, then continued diamonds.

Tush was a dead duck; he had good cards in hearts and clubs now, but had fallen behind in trump length, and could win only his remaining high trumps. Down three for –500 North-South, against the par of –140 for 3♡ by the opposition.

The full deal had been:

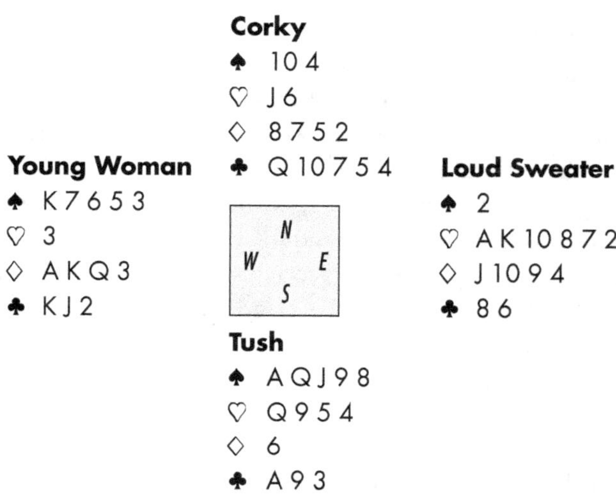

"Nice defense," said Tush. "Nothing I could do."

"You *could*, I suppose, draw trumps and knock out the ace of hearts," suggested Loud Sweater mildly. "That holds it to –300."

Tush flushed. Draw trumps and concede down two? Can that have been the right thing to do? It seemed so. Bridge 101. Damn! Could he have recovered by attacking hearts instead of clubs? No, East would have forced him with diamonds, and if he tried to pitch his losers on the diamonds, the defense would conclude by ruffing his ♡Q. Wait— didn't East chuck her fourth-round diamond entry at Trick 3? But even if she holds onto it, Tush realized, he could wait and ruff the last *diamond*, then draw trumps and play the ♡Q, endplaying West in clubs. Yes, there were lots of ways to get out for down two, only one way not to. Tush opened his mouth to suggest moving on to the next deal, but too late—Corky was already speaking.

"Even better," she said, one eyebrow raised, "might be to stay out of the bidding. They were headed for game, down. That would have been five IMPs for us, instead of eight for them."

"Hey, give me a break," Tush huffed. "I had a good hand! You might have had another trump or two for me, you know. I had long hearts, so you figured to be short in hearts, thus likely long in spades."

"Oh, Robert, Robert," Corky sighed. "That old fallacy? Come on. By that reasoning, isn't West also likely to have more spades? And how about East? He presumably has fewer hearts than expected for his response, since you have four, so shouldn't he have more spades on average, too?"

Tush paused. Corky had a point; his argument seemed to make it more likely that *everyone* had more spades. But there were eight spades out, no more, no less, so how could that be?

"I still don't see what's wrong with my reasoning. Surely, my being long in their suit makes it more likely that you are short. And, surely, your being short in their suit makes it more likely that you are long in mine. Which of these statements is wrong?"

"They're both right, it's the conclusion that's wrong," said Corky. "The fact that A makes B more likely, and B makes C more likely, doesn't mean that A makes C more likely."

"It doesn't? Are you sure?"

"Absolutely. I'm not sure I can come up with an example on the fly, but..."

"How about this one," said Loud Sweater. "Pick a random American. If he's black, is he more likely to live in a southern state?"

"Yes, somewhat more likely, I suppose," said Tush dubiously.

"And if a random American is from a southern state, isn't he more likely to have voted for McCain in the 2008 presidential election?"

"Well, yes, McCain did carry most of the southern states."

"So, is a black American more likely to have voted for McCain?"

Tush tried to put this together. 'A' was being black, 'B' living in a southern state, 'C' having voted for McCain. It seemed to work; certainly a black American was not more likely to have voted for McCain. Tush knew that Obama had gotten a huge black majority. But Tush couldn't seem to get it all into his head at the same time. "Listen," he said exasperatedly. "I don't know much about racial politics, but it seems to me I've seen this reasoning about trump length in print. I didn't make it up. And I'm still not convinced. I figured my partner has two hearts at most, and indeed she did have only two. So isn't it a bit unlucky that she also had a doubleton spade?"

"Here's another way to look at it," said West. "Because you're long in hearts, you have fewer minor-suit cards. So your partner has more minor-suit cards. So, fewer spades."

Tush was getting seriously frustrated. "So now you're telling me that she's *less* likely to have spade support?"

"No, no, just that the same reasoning applies to all the non-spades in your hand. It doesn't matter how those eight cards are distributed among the three remaining suits; the expected number of spades in your partner's hand is unaffected."

Time for a new defense, thought Tush. "Okay, forget about my long hearts," he said. "Surely, I'm not supposed to let you sit there and conduct a nine-round relay auction, when I'm non-vulnerable with a nice hand?"

Corky and the opponents looked at one other, sighs all around. "Do you want to do this, or shall I?" offered Corky.

West turned to Tush. "First of all, you shouldn't be afraid of letting us relay. We're no more likely to get to the right contract than standard bidders of equal skill, believe me. The main advantage we have, playing natural relays, is that it's easier than standard two-way communication, and can be done with fewer partnership agreements."

"Actually," East contributed, "relayers too often fail to break out of a relay auction when it becomes apparent that they aren't going to get the right information. Pure laziness. Also, they force to game too early; in this board, there was no way for us to avoid a poor game."

"Secondly," West continued, "it's dangerous to interfere with a relay auction. When you jump into a standard auction, it takes a certain amount of cooperation for the opponents to know when to double. But, in a relay auction, one of the opponents has all the information and the other will happily go along."

"Plus," said East, "especially against natural relayers like us, if you don't bid high, it's hard to mess us up. In the actual auction, if my partner had wanted to relay instead of doubling you, she'd have passed, and my bid options would be the same as if you hadn't overcalled; except that with (relatively) good spades I could make a natural penalty double."

"And, of course, the more you bid, the better we know how to play the hand," said West. "Either you get punished, or we get rewarded."

Tush's mind was now in a total whirl. "I thought relays were fantastically effective, extremely difficult to use, and mandatory to interfere with whenever possible," said Tush. "Are you trying to tell me that *all* of these impressions are wrong?"

"Not merely wrong," laughed Loud Sweater. "Ass backwards!"

"Last week," said West, "we were headed for a bad slam when one of our opponents decided to double a relay for a lead. Turns out, he would have been on lead himself. Anyway, it went pass, pass, redouble. Chad brought it home nicely on a 5–1 fit, 7 IMPs. Very satisfying."

"Hey," said Tush. "What about those relay pairs who used to dominate the bidding contests in *The Bridge World* magazine? Those systems were complicated and effective, with no opponents to interfere."

"Number one," countered West, "deals in *Challenge the Champs* are chosen to be difficult to handle with standard methods. Number two, they are often in the slam or grand slam zone. Number three, pairs who put in as much work on their slam bidding as these pairs did on their relay auctions also do very well."

"To be fair," added East, "*our* system gives up some accuracy in order to be easy and fun to play. But jumping into an artificial relay auction is no better. If the relayers have a well-thought-out system, they will know what to do when you come in. My advice: stay out unless your hand is screaming for a sacrifice."

X X X

After East and West left the table, Tush turned to Corky. "No doubt, your regular partner wouldn't have fallen into this trap?"

"Probably not, if you must know."

"Too bad about his reliability problem, eh?" It was a mean thing to say, but Tush couldn't stop himself.

"*She* is an ER physician, and sometimes has to back out of commitments at the last minute. A fact I should learn to accept better than I have, I'm afraid."

Something about the way she said that... "She's not just your bridge partner, is she?"

"Very good, Robert."

"I'm sorry, I guess I was a bit insensitive there."

"No, it's all right. I'm grateful to you for substituting today. You're really a good player. Sometimes things don't go as well as they should."

Amen to that, thought Tush. So much for his daydreams about Corky.

TUSH MISSES A DUCK

Dean and Glenda were the next opponents—another Ricochet pair, Tush thought gloomily. Worse, they seem to have kissed and made up since the deal where Glenda raised to 3NT with a septuple stopper. Now they looked sharp and ready.

Holding

♠ K 9 8 2   ♡ A Q J 4   ◇ 6 4   ♣ 1 0 8 6

Tush saw two passes and added a third. West (Dean) opened with 1NT, 13-15 HCP, BALANCED. Corky passed and Glenda bid 3♡, SPLINTER, which Tush somewhat recklessly doubled. The bidding continued 4◇ 4♡ by Corky, and 5◇, ending the auction.

West	North	East	South
Dean	Corky	Glenda	Tush
	pass	pass	pass
1NT	pass	3♡	dbl
4◇	4♡	5◇	all pass

Corky led the ♡9, and dummy came down.

Contract: 5◇ by West
Opening lead: ♡9

Dummy
♠ Q 6 5 3
♡ 6
◇ Q J 8
♣ A Q J 9 5

N
W   E
S

Tush
♠ K 9 8 2
♡ A Q J 4
◇ 6 4
♣ 10 8 6

The table was pretty strong, Tush thought, for a passed hand, but he remembered that Ricochet players liked to have an ace and a king to open the bidding. There was another feature of the hand that surprised him, though—the lack of a fourth trump.

"Can I ask a you a question about the bidding?" he said to East. "I'm just curious—I haven't tried splinters over notrump. But shouldn't you have bid five clubs with that hand? Couldn't your partner be, like, three-three-four-three?"

Glenda held out her hands palms upward. "And your point is…?"

"Um, a four-three fit at the five-level?" Tush persisted.

"Let's see how it plays, shall we?"

Declarer played the ♡3 under Tush's ace, and Tush stopped to consider. Apparently declarer had king–ten left in hearts, and would probably be ruffing the ten on the board and then tackling trumps. The king would stop the hearts if declarer had only four trumps and had to give up one. Then clubs would be run. Yuck.

Could declarer be missing the ♠A? Unlikely—for one thing, Corky might have led the ace from ♠Ax or a trump from a bunch of small ones. But Tush couldn't imagine any other way to beat the hand, so he switched to a spade.

Indeed, there was nothing Tush could do. The full deal was:

   Bridge at the Enigma Club

Corky
♠ J 7
♡ 9 8 7 5 2
♢ A 5 3 2
♣ 7 2

Dean
♠ A 10 4
♡ K 10 3
♢ K 10 9 7
♣ K 4 3

Glenda
♠ Q 6 5 3
♡ 6
♢ Q J 8
♣ A Q J 9 5

Tush
♠ K 9 8 2
♡ A Q J 4
♢ 6 4
♣ 10 8 6

Declarer ran Tush's spade return to the board's queen, forced out the ace of trumps (taken by Corky on the third round), drew the remaining trump, and claimed.

Tush sighed and turned to dummy apologetically. "All right, I admit it, that was a nice spot," he said. "All other game contracts are miserable. Too bad all you get is zero IMPs against par."

"Actually," said Glenda, examining the table display, "we seem to be getting ten IMPs. Par is just +140 our way."

Tush stared. "We can beat this? How? Maybe if my partner leads a trump…?"

"Hey," said Corky, "don't blame me! You're the one who put up the ace of hearts. If I lead a trump, and you later go up ace on a heart lead, it's just as bad."

Tush shook his head. "What are you talking about? You want me to duck the ace of hearts on the opening lead? And let him win his king opposite the stiff on the board? Are you serious?"

But even as he said this, the light began to dawn on Tush. Without his king of hearts, declarer was up the creek without a paddle. If he went after trumps, before or after ruffing a heart or two on the board, Corky would hold up her ace until dummy's trumps were exhausted, then force declarer in hearts.

Funny, thought Tush, if declarer had had the ♡A instead of the king, he would have needed to let Tush hold the opening lead—a good, but not extraordinary play. With the king… "Wait, can't declarer duck too?"

"Then you can shift, or just continue underleading in hearts," said Corky. "As long as you keep that ace of hearts, he's dead. Actually, I think you can even play *small* on my opening lead and let him make his ten; he's still doomed. Anything but the ace—"

"Okay already! Yipes, I miss a double-dummy duck and everyone gets excited. Sheesh!" But, Tush was thinking: if he had devoted as much thought to the defense before he played the ace as he had afterward, would he have found this play?

TUSH OVERLOOKS A THIRD OPTION

On the next board, Tush picked up the following modest collection:

♠ 10 7 5   ♡ 10 8 7 2   ◇ Q J 10 4   ♣ 9 3

After Glenda and he passed, his left-hand opponent, Dean, began with a forcing club. East responded 1◇,

NEGATIVE, FEWER THAN 9 HCP

and West jumped to 2♠. This was raised to three by East, and West concluded the auction by bidding the spade game.

West	North	East	South
Dean	Corky	Glenda	Tush
		pass	pass
1♣	pass	1◇	pass
2♠	pass	3♠	pass
4♠	all pass		

Corky led the ♡K, and when dummy came down Tush noted that his own hand had not been the worst at the table.

Contract: 4♠ by West
Opening lead: ♡K

Dummy

♠ 9 8 3
♡ Q 6 5 4
◇ 9 8 2
♣ 8 7 2

Tush

♠ 10 7 5
♡ 10 8 7 2
◇ Q J 10 4
♣ 9 3

Declarer ruffed the opening lead, cashed the ♣A and ♣K, Corky following with the five and four, and continued with the ♣6 to Corky's jack. Tush was prepared to pitch a small heart, but paused: it was tempting to ruff instead, and fire the ◇Q through declarer.

But could this really do any good? Could declarer hold ◇Kxx, planning to pitch a diamond from the board on a good club? Or on a bad club, trying to endplay Corky? That wouldn't work, since Tush could ruff the *next* club.

Not able to see any great advantage in ruffing, Tush discarded a heart. Corky continued with the ♣Q, declarer throwing a diamond from the board, and again Tush was tempted to ruff; but, on reflection, it seemed as if Corky would always be able to exit safely with a trump or the ♡A. So why waste a trump? Tush threw another heart.

Declarer followed with a small club, won Corky's trump jack in hand, and led a diamond himself. Tush's ten won the defense's third trick, and he got out with a small trump. Declarer won, cashed the ◇A, ruffed a diamond on the board, ruffed a heart back to his hand and claimed the rest with good trumps in hand.

The full deal lit up on the table.

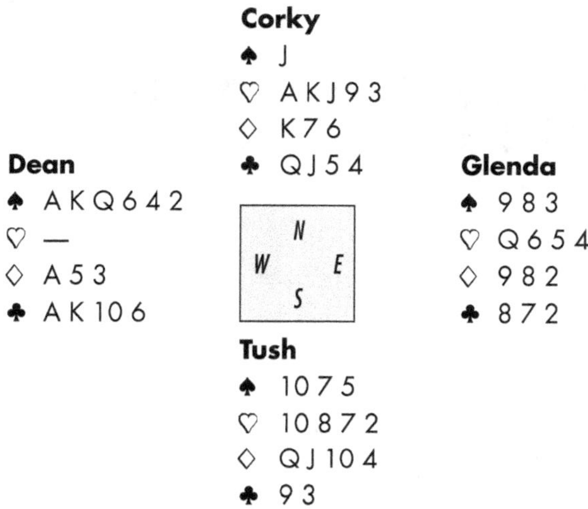

Par was −500 to North-South for four hearts doubled, down two. "As a sacrifice against three notrump by East-West," Corky observed. "A diamond lead beats the spade game. Too tough for me."

"I thought about ruffing your good club and leading a diamond through," said Tush, "but it just makes things easier for declarer— he can even draw trumps now and ruff his fourth club instead of a diamond."

But as he said this, a horrifying thought rose up into Tush's brain like foul air from a sinkhole. If he had pitched a *diamond* on Corky's ♣J, and then another on the queen, he could have overruffed the board. Yes, all he had to do was to keep pace with dummy's diamond shortness. Arrgh!

Corky's voice penetrated his thoughts. "Are you okay?"

"Er—yes, fine. Just wondering to myself whether I'd have found that nice play by Dean." Actually, Tush saw, declarer could have made the contract legitimately after the heart lead, by running trumps, then ducking a diamond; squeeze and endplay against Corky. But maybe the less said about this deal, the better.

The table lit up, signaling the end of the round. Not a moment too soon, thought Tush.

TUSH FAILS TO DRAW TRUMP

The two well-dressed women were Tush's new opponents, not looking as grim as last time. Why was it that everyone seemed to be doing better than Tush and Corky? Hmm, one of them was now towing a bespectacled child of perhaps ten years.

"Do you mind if my daughter kibitzes? She's learning to play, and knows to speak only when spoken to. Right, Charlene?"

The child grinned to reveal a colorful array of food particles in a jungle of braces. "Yes, Ma."

"Um, I guess it's okay," said Tush, with a sharp glance at Corky, hoping for some kind of rescue. But Corky only shrugged; what could she say, anyway?

With Charlene's pungent breath in his left ear, Tush gazed upon

♠ K Q J 10 9   ♡ 5 4 2   ♢ A   ♣ 10 9 6 5

as dealer. His shaded 1♠ opening drew a jump to 3NT from partner, which could only have been the previously-reviled classic response showing a flat 16-17. Or did it show just two trumps these days? No matter, with a singleton, strong trumps and no thoughts of slam, Tush corrected to 4♠.

West	North	East	South
			1♠
pass	3NT	pass	4♠
all pass			

Charlene's mother put the $\diamondsuit$Q on the table, and Corky spread a hand that made Tush happy he had not sat for 3NT.

Contract: 4♠ by South
Opening lead: $\diamondsuit$Q

Dummy
♠ A 7 3
♡ A J 7 6
$\diamondsuit$ 8 7 4
♣ A Q J

Tush
♠ K Q J 10 9
♡ 5 4 2
$\diamondsuit$ A
♣ 10 9 6 5

Tush won the lead with his stiff ace, East following with the $\diamondsuit$6, then Tush played a trump to the board's ace and back to his king. On this, West discarded a diamond.

The 4-1 trump break gave Tush pause. If he pulled the remaining trump, the club blockage could give him problems. Instead, keeping the trump entry to hand, he played a club to the queen.

East won her king and led a diamond back. Tush ruffed and led a club to the ace, with the intent of returning to hand in trumps, discarding the blocking ♣J on his last trump, and claiming.

Alas, East ruffed the ♣A and returned another small diamond. Tush had to ruff this, else suffer another club ruff by East. But now, with no long trump on which to unload the ♣J, he couldn't even hold the damage to down one.

Corky
♠ A 7 3
♡ A J 7 6
◇ 8 7 4
♣ A Q J

♠ 4   ♠ 8 6 5 2
♡ K 8   ♡ Q 10 9 3
◇ Q J 10 9 5   ◇ K 6 3 2
♣ 8 7 4 3 2   ♣ K

Tush
♠ K Q J 10 9
♡ 5 4 2
◇ A
♣ 10 9 6 5

"Rabbi's Rule would have saved me," said Tush, unwisely. "But if I go up ace, her singleton will be a small one."

This Corky could not resist. "If you go up ace after drawing trump, you always make."

"I don't believe you. What if they win the second round of clubs and play diamonds?"

"No problem, you just sluff hearts from hand. If they persist with a fourth round, pitch dummy's high club on it, ruff and claim."

My God, thought Tush, did I miss a one-hundred-percent line? But before he could fully absorb this blow, West spoke up.

"Charlene, did you hear that?"

"Yes, Ma."

"And what lesson did we learn?"

"Always draw trump."

"Very good, Charlene!" and to Tush: "Isn't she something?"

TUSH IS DISTRACTED BY A QUEEN

Fourth in hand, vulnerable against not, Tush picked up a nice-looking major-suiter:

♠ A Q 10 9 2   ♡ A K Q 4   ◇ 9 7 6   ♣ 2

The bidding began with a Ricochet 1◇, 11-15 HCP, 4+ DIAMONDS.

West	North	East	South
1◇	pass	1♡	1♠
pass	1NT	pass	2♡
pass	2♣	pass	3♠
pass	4♠	all pass	

West led the ♣K and Tush considered this landscape:

Contract: 4♠ by South
Opening lead: ♣K

Dummy
♠ J 7
♡ 3 2
◇ A 5 4 3
♣ Q 10 9 7 6

Tush
♠ A Q 10 9 2
♡ A K Q 4
◇ 9 7 6
♣ 2

Four spades again, and there would be no hundred-percent line on this one, that was for sure. But Tush was complicit in reaching this shaky game; he'd better make the best of it. Well, if he could ruff a heart and find king-doubleton of trumps on his right, he was home. Not much, but what else was there?

Accordingly, he won West's ◇K shift with the ace, cashed ace–king of hearts and continued with a small one. West threw a club; Tush ruffed and led the board's last trump to his queen, holding the trick. So far, so good.

But nobody played the ♠K under Tush's ace. Down one. The hands were:

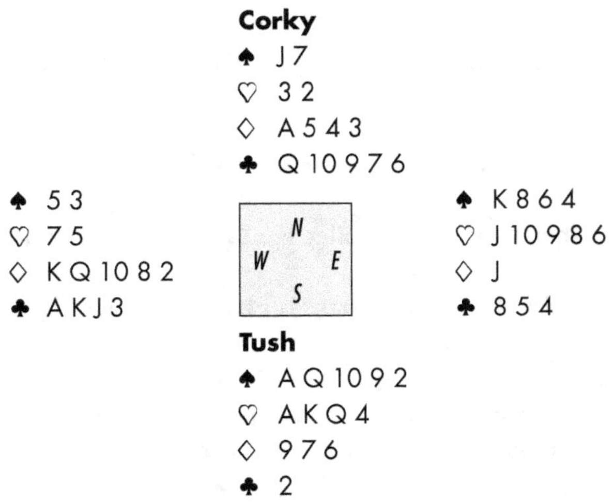

Par was +140 for North-South, 6 IMPs away.

"I'm afraid I was a little light for my bidding," Tush conceded.

"Maybe you should have been a little lighter," said Corky. "Replace your queen of hearts with the deuce, and you'd probably have made the game."

"What are you talking about? I took a trick with that card!"

"Look at the deal, and tell me what you would do if you had only ace–king and two small hearts, after the club lead and diamond shift."

"Not much different. I ruff *two* hearts on the board, getting back to hand with club ruffs. Now I need to drop the king of trumps singleton. Same outcome."

"Not if you ruff clubs in your hand whenever you can. Try again."

Tush mentally ruffed a club at Trick 3, cashed ace–king of hearts and crossruffed hearts and clubs. After the ninth trick, Tush would be down to ♠AQ ♡— ◇97 ♣—. Now he would exit with a diamond, and wait to make his two trumps.

"Okay," said Tush, "But what's to prevent me doing the same thing with the hand I actually held?"

"Exactly," said Corky. "Two top hearts, two heart ruffs, three club ruffs, ace of diamonds and ace–queen of trump makes ten tricks."

An awful feeling of déjà vu descended upon Tush—yes, only a dozen or so boards ago, Corky herself had been victimized by a superfluous high card. But she had seen the error herself. Tush had needed to have it spelled out. He felt a spreading blackness within.

A few seconds of silence followed, during which East started to gather her things. But West was not quite ready to go.

"Well, Charlene? What lesson did we learn this time?"

The child knitted her unibrow in concentration. "Always count your tricks?"

"Isn't she amazing?" said West, beaming. Tush couldn't stand it.

"If you really want to know—"

"Indeed she is," Corky interrupted quickly. "An expert in the making!"

X X X

"That was a rhetorical question, Robert," said Corky after the opponents departed. "Please, take it easy. You're getting very agitated. Do you realize your fists are clenched?"

TUSH REFUSES TO GO QUIETLY

Tush was still taking controlled breaths when the two professorial types took their seats, in deep conversation concerning the previous board. "I hope I'm finding a trump or a diamond lead if they get to game," said Beard. "I think they can bring it home if I start with a top club."

Indeed they can, thought Tush, gritting his teeth. But, he needed to put that out of mind. Helping matters was the attractive display of royalty before Tush's eyes:

♠ A Q 5   ♡ Q 10 6   ◇ A K 5 2   ♣ K Q 8

Corky passed as dealer, but before Tush could open 2NT, Mustache beat him to the punch with a 1♡ opener on Tush's right. With this information came the words:

ALERT: MAY BE A CONTROLLED PSYCHIC

Interesting. Well, psychic or no, Tush had a takeout double.
West bid 1NT and now the alert said:

10+ HCP AND THE ACE OR KING OF OPENER'S SUIT

Uh oh, thought Tush—this smacks of crypto. Indeed, after Corky's pass, East's bid of 2♣ showed:

Tush turned to his left-hand opponent. "I suppose two diamonds would have shown the opposite?"

"Right. Without the ace or king, he bids something else, and then presumably has a real opener. He wouldn't psych without one of the top two of his suit—it's supposed to direct a lead."

"But as it is, you know if his opener was genuine, and I don't, isn't that the idea?"

"Exactly."

"Now, let me get this straight. In ACBL events, psychics are frowned upon, and frequent psychics a cause for disciplinary action. Controlled psychics are illegal, everywhere. And this is no ordinary controlled psychic, it's crypto-controlled. You get to 'catch' it, I don't. So, really, this should be a capital offence, by my reckoning."

"Robert, ease off," said Corky. "It's only a game."

"We're a private club, you know," said East. "And crypto is perfectly legal within the laws of bridge. If there weren't directors like P-G who allow experimentation, how would the game advance?"

Tush was tired of arguing. "Okay, I give up. Forget it. Let's play."

Now he had to make a call, but 2NT was ludicrously dangerous even at favorable vulnerability. Plus, psychic or not on his right, lefty could be loaded. But he could hardly pass; Corky and he could easily have a game. He doubled again.

WEST	NORTH	EAST	SOUTH
	PASS	1♡	DBL
1NT	PASS	2♣	DBL
2♡	PASS	PASS	

Back to Tush. Tush knew he should pass now. This was IMPs. But he had 20 points. Game was unlikely and he had a defensive-looking hand. But in his current state of mind Tush couldn't sit there and let them play in 2♡, undoubled and untroubled. He doubled yet again.

The full auction and deal:

West	**North**	**East**	**South**
Beard	Corky	Mustache	Tush
	pass	1♡	dbl
1NT	pass	2♣	dbl
2♡	pass	pass	dbl
pass	2♠	pass	pass
dbl	all pass		

Contract: 2♠ doubled, by North
Opening lead: ◇3

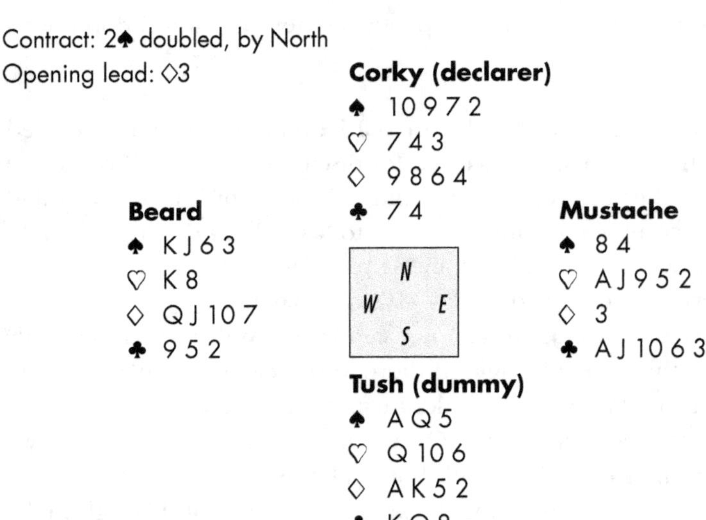

Corky (declarer)
♠ 10 9 7 2
♡ 7 4 3
◇ 9 8 6 4
♣ 7 4

Beard
♠ K J 6 3
♡ K 8
◇ Q J 10 7
♣ 9 5 2

Mustache
♠ 8 4
♡ A J 9 5 2
◇ 3
♣ A J 10 6 3

Tush (dummy)
♠ A Q 5
♡ Q 10 6
◇ A K 5 2
♣ K Q 8

So East was legit. That was 500 away, with no game East-West; par was 140 their way for a heart partial. Tush knew it was his own fault. He knew other Souths would be getting in trouble, too, but that was small solace for forcing his innocent partner to play a hopeless doubled contract.

TUSH ENCOUNTERS ROSENCRYPT

Exasperated beyond words, Tush pushed the 1◊ button in second position, with

♠ 10 9 4 3   ♡ K J 10 5   ◊ A K 4 2   ♣ A

Beard overcalled 1♠. No alert—hallelujah!

Corky raised to 2◊, and Mustache doubled, alerted as:

```
ROSENCRYPT: SHOWS ONE OF THE TOP 2 CARDS
IN OVERCALLER'S SUIT.
```

"Shouldn't that be Rosenkranz?" Tush asked Beard, but he knew the answer as soon as the question escaped his lips.

"It is Rosenkranz. The only difference is, we use it to set up key for encryption, as well as marking an opening lead. Why waste the opportunity? If we don't use it later in the bidding, we still have it for the defense. We signal normally if his top spade is the ace, upside-down if it's the king."

Tush rolled his eyes up toward heaven. These guys were in another universe, for sure.

Looking back at his own hand, Tush saw pleasing defensive values. Could he nail them at the three-level? Get some revenge for the previous board? Appealing to his own last shred of optimism, he raised the stakes to the level of 3◊. It went pass, pass, 3♠. The auction had been:

West	North	East	South
Beard	Corky	Mustache	Tush
		pass	1◇
1♠	2◇	dbl	3◇
pass	pass	3♠	?

Tush looked down for his DOUBLE button, but the 3♠ call had come with a message: competitive with trump ace, invitational with king.

Tush looked up at West.

"Three hearts would have had the reverse meaning," Beard explained.

Tush had no wish to double a game try. "So, which is it?" he demanded hotly. "Competitive or invitational?"

"Robert, please," whispered Corky.

"If he has the spade ace—"

"*Which is it?*"

X X X

Tush had only vague memories of what transpired after that. P-G showed up with two other massive individuals, there was some sort of struggle, and sometime after that Tush was climbing out of a cab in front of his hotel.

The next morning he was on his flight home. He had never gotten Corky's last name, or anyone's, for that matter. Or the name of the club. Or even the name of the street it was on. To be fair, his head hurt, and he wasn't trying very hard to remember the details.

EPILOG

"My name's Robert Tischman—your team knocked mine out of the Spingold, at the Summer Nationals?"

"Ah yes, I remember. You put up a good fight, though. I didn't know you were from these parts."

"I'm not, actually. Just flew in for a conference." In fact, this was Tush's first time back since that fateful afternoon a year and a half ago. He had already spent a day making fruitless inquiries at a publicly-advertised local bridge club, and searching on foot for a familiar carved building. Now, he was reduced to looking up a local expert he hardly knew and begging for a coffee shop rendezvous. "I really must thank you again for agreeing to meet me. I won't keep you long, and you're welcome to another macchiato on me, of course."

"This'll do. You said you were looking for a club you once played at?"

"Yes, but unfortunately I don't remember where it was exactly, except on the fourth floor of some oldish building downtown. The director was called 'P-G' but I didn't get anyone's last name."

"Hmm, doesn't ring a bell. Are you sure it was a regular club?"

Tush laughed. "If you mean, did it meet regularly, I got the impression that they had a two-session duplicate every Saturday. But they were not your usual bridge club, at least not where I come from. Among other things, they had high-tech tables with touch screen bidding and automatic computer dealing. Each deal was played at every table at the same time. And they scored IMPs against double-dummy par."

"Seriously? Does that even make sense?"

"They seemed to think so. And that's not all. They made heavy use of cryptologic techniques, and some relay system they call Ricochet."

"Cryptologic techniques? As in secret codes? Wait a minute, that rings a bell—yes, someone once told me there was a weekly game in town at something called the Enigma Club. But I've never been there, and don't know anyone who has."

"Hmm," Tush mused. "Wasn't Enigma the name of that German cipher machine broken by the Allies?"

"Yes, that's the one. But, you know, encrypted signaling is expressly forbidden for tournament play by the ACBL."

"It's not just signaling they use encryption for. Opening leads, cuebidding, defensive bidding, psychic controls, you name it. I think this P-G used to work for the National Security Agency, and some of the players, too."

"Have you tried calling the NSA?"

"Yeah, right."

"Okay, more seriously, did you do a web search on cryptology in bridge? Or on, what was it, 'Ricochet?' If this is a relay system, there's probably a thousand pages of unfathomable notes on it published somewhere."

"No luck there. And anyway, Ricochet is a 'natural' relay system, it's actually supposed to be easier to play than Standard American. It's based on certain general principles, like the idea that you always have a neutral response available when partner forces. It uses a big club, but it has some weird features like non-forcing two-over-one."

"Well, you know there have been many attempts to come up with unified bidding systems, but they never catch on."

Tush shrugged. "This one seems to have caught on only at the 'Enigma Club,' if that's really what its name is."

"Why are you looking for it, anyway? Sounds pretty off-the-wall to me."

"I don't know, I did learn some interesting things there. Did you know there are more possible auctions than possible deals?"

"Is that so?"

"Check it out. How about this: ever get caught in a one-card squeeze?"

"You're kidding, right?"

"And, did you ever reason that because you're long in the opponents' suit, that your partner is probably short there, thus is likely to have support for your suit?"

"Sure, what's wrong with that?"

"It's a crock. Have you ever had the dubious pleasure of defending three notrump with declarer's hand completely unknown?"

"Well, maybe not completely, but..."

"Happens all the time in this club. As do a lot of curious things."

"Are you sure you didn't just dream this whole thing?"

"Sometimes I wonder. Oh well, like I said, I do appreciate your help. If I ever do find the club, I'll email you."

"Thanks. Sorry I couldn't have been more help. See you next Nationals?"

"I hope so. Thanks again. Take care." Tush picked up the check as the expert got up to leave. "Wait, one more question. Did you ever notice that six diamonds always makes?"

The expert turned around, coat in hand, to face Tush. "For heaven's sake, Robert, *everyone* knows *that.*"

NOTES AND SOURCES

CRYPTO

Cryptologic techniques in bidding and defense were introduced by this author in a series of articles in *The Bridge World* and *Bridge Magazine* [see Bibliography: 26, 27, 28, 29, 30, 31, 32]. At

http://www.blakjak.demon.co.uk/brx_win1.htm

the latter series can be found, as of this writing. A more mathematical article [Bibliography: 34] followed shortly; the same journal published "Bridge Cryptography Fundamentals" [18] as recently as 2006.

The application to defensive signaling had been anticipated by several UK bridge writers, including the late Albert Benjamin of Scotland [3], Mike Tedd of Wales, and Peter Copping of England. The latter wrote in 1980 an (apparently unpublished) article about a signal, naturally called the Copping Peter, which utilized "the reversing of signals in certain situations when declarer cannot read the position."

Reaction to encrypted methods was immediate in Europe. *The Bridge Magazine* articles were solicited for translation into German, and the final article [32]—a first-person short story along the lines of this book—was translated into Dutch and published on the Web. (Later it was translated back to English and reposted, losing quite a few nuances in the process.)

Encrypted signaling got a publicity boost stateside from Alan Truscott in three *New York Times* bridge columns [19, 20, 21], the last calling it "one of the most ingenious thoughts in the area of defense in recent years." Interest reached sufficient proportions for the American Contract Bridge League to ban encrypted signaling from league-sanctioned tournaments worldwide, effective May 4, 1987 (and still on the books). Numerous other bridge organizations have banned encrypted signals, encrypted calls, or both. These regulations have no effect, of course, on international competition, and encrypted signals have been used by the Taiwanese national team.

Encryption in bridge has occasionally reached outside the game. For pedagogic purposes, Deborah Bennett, author of *Logic Made Easy*[4], cites conditionals (a general logical technique) as "the tactic used by mathematician Peter Winkler to confound his opponents with his infamous methods of bidding and signaling in the game of bridge." Professors Michael Fisher of Yale and Rebecca Wright of Rutgers [6, 7] used the bridge idea to show how a group of people could distribute a key for private communication using a virtual deck of cards. Finally, in [2, 14] the general notion of constructing a cryptographic key from common knowledge was abstracted.

RICOCHET

Ricochet—more of an idea for a system than a fleshed-out system—was devised by the author, with experimental help from four indulgent partners: Dave Kelly, Atlanta GA; Matt Franklin, Berkeley CA; Graham Brightwell, London UK; and Chris Storm, New York City.

Our experiences with Ricochet were often profitable and always entertaining. Since it is a big club system, similar in many auctions to Precision, it is susceptible to interference after 1♣ openings and often generates swings for the mundane reason of having different notrump ranges from Standard American. However, we got many additional good results by playing 3NT by unknown hands and by having our opening diamond bids actually show diamonds. Other bonanzas came from opponents who (like Tush) thought they had to interfere with relay auctions, and—amazingly often—from opponents who could not reach their makeable game after we opened 1♣. Ricochet's non-forcing 2/1 and freewheeling style put us in the thick of partscore battles, but to get the best out of the system for bidding strong hands, much more work and detail would be required.

The main distinguishing features of Ricochet are the relays and neutrals. Any unlimited hand has an artificial forcing "relay" available— usually, the lowest bid that isn't a logical slam, game or twobelow. (Recall that a "twobelow" is a bid two below game, namely 1NT, 2 of a major or 3 of a minor.) The most important relays are the opening 1♣, the 1NT response to other one-level opening bids, and the takeout double (after the latter, cuebids are relays). Responses to Ricochet relays are natural, except for the neutral response, and the one-level responses to 1♣.

Any forced hand has a neutral response available—again, usually the lowest bid that isn't a logical slam, game or twobelow. If right-hand opponent relieves the force by bidding, doubling or redoubling, "pass" is (as in standard bidding) the neutral response; the difference in Ricochet is that even when the guy on your right doesn't cooperate, you still have a way to say "nothing to say."

Relays and neutrals, as defined here, are hardly exclusive to Ricochet. For example, 2♣ Stayman is a relay and the standard 2◇ response is neutral. Many expert pairs play reverses by opener as relays, with an agreed-upon neutral response. The difference is that Ricochet tries to make relays and neutrals a universal principle. However, our experience suggests that while relaying is fun, most unbalanced strong hands should break out of relay sequences early in order to get the right information from partner.

The following is an outline of the Ricochet system. You can of course substitute your favorite system over notrump openings, for example, or defensive conventions, for what you see below. Encrypted raises, with rotated cuebids, are included, but the reader is reminded that crypto features are independent of Ricochet; either is usable without the other. The system as presented here was used by a casual partnership in tournament play; it would need to be simplified for presentation to a novice class, and augmented for an expert partnership.

Indentation is used to indicate successive bids by the two Ricochet partners, with opener's bids in italic.

CONSTRUCTIVE BIDDING

Principles of 1♣ auctions:

- Opener may relay (with cheapest suit bid) as long as desired, after which bidding is natural.
- First response at one-level is negative or suitless; at two-level or higher, decent suits of five cards or more.
- Responder shows shape first, then concentration of strength. After opener sets suit, responder cuebids controls, or jumps to show singletons.
- Notrump by opener at first opportunity shows 16-18, after one relay 19-21, after two 22-24 etc.; system on unless responder has shown a suit.
- Notrump bids by responder, before opener has bid NT, show specific numbers of kinks (a kink is a king or half of an A Q combination).

1♣: relay, ≥16 HCP, any shape
  1◇: neutral, <9 HCP
    1♡: relay (strong)
      1♠: neutral, <6 HCP
        1NT: 19–21 HCP, balanced (system on)
        2♣: relay (very strong)
          2◇: neutral
          2NT: one king
          other: natural
        other: natural, not forcing
      1NT: two kinks (two kings or one A Q combination)
      other: natural, game force
    1♠, 2♣, 2◇, 2♡: natural, not forcing
    1NT: 16–18 HCP, balanced (system on)
  1♡, no long suit, ≥9 HCP, ≤3 controls (A = 2 controls, K = 1)
  1♠, no long suit, ≥9 HCP, ≥4 controls
  1NT: three kinks (three kings or one king and one A Q combo),
    balanced, game force
  2♣, 2◇, 2♡, 2♠: ≥ five-card suit, ≥9 HCP, game force
  2NT: balanced, four kinks (rare!)
  3 of a suit: ≥ six-card good suit, game force

Principles of auctions beginning 1X (X = ◇, ♡ or ♠):

- Raise structure is the same in all three suits: 2NT limit raise or better, at least one of top three trumps; 3NT, forcing and at least two of top three trumps; splinters.
- With all strong hands other than raises, responder relays with 1NT. Responder can continue relaying with cheapest suit bids (skipping bids in X).
- With a strong raise not suitable for 2NT, 3NT or splinter, responder may bid 1NT followed by non-jump in X, invitational. Other suit continuations by 1NT responder are game forcing.
- Raise to 2X (X a major) may be made on honor-doubleton and as much as 10 HCP; jump to 3X preemptive, could be only three trumps and a singleton; jump to 4X to play, big range.
- 2/1 not forcing (as if by passed hand).
- Single jumps are fit-jumps, good suit plus three-card fit in X, forcing to 3X.

Bridge at the Enigma Club

1X (X = ◇, ♡ or ♠): 11–15 HCP, unbalanced, ≥ five cards of named major suit and, for the 1◇ opening, at least four diamonds
    1NT: relay (except by passed hand, when it is 10-12 HCP, balanced)
        2♣: neutral; other: natural
            cheapest suit call other than in X: relay
            minimum call in X: invitational
            jump in X, short of game: flawed forcing raise (not eligible for 2NT)
            2NT: strongly invitational
            other: game force
    new suit at 1-level: ≥ four cards, forcing for one round
    new suit at 2-level: ≥ five cards, not forcing
    2X: ≥ two-card support, 7-10 HCP (3+ if X = diamonds)
    2NT: limit raise or better, with A, K or Q of trump
        3 of new suit, below 3X: natural, probing for game
        3X: to play
        3NT: slam interest, missing a high trump
        4 of new suit: encrypted cues begin
        4X: good playing hand, weak in controls
        4NT: Blackwood, but trump ace doesn't count!
    3X: ≥ three-card support, 0-6 HCP, preemptive (vulnerability a factor!)
    jump in new suit: fit-jump, ≥3 support, forcing to 3X
    3NT: forcing raise, two of the top three trumps
        4 of new suit: encrypted cue
        4X: weak, to play
        4NT: slam interest, but no high trump
    double jump in new suit: splinter
    jump to game in X: to play, 0-15 HCP(!), ≥ 3 trumps.

Principle of notrump auctions: system on if (a) partner of notrump bidder has not already bid a suit naturally, and (b) LHO of notrump bidder passes, doubles artificially, or bids 2♣ (in which case DBL becomes Stayman).

1NT: 13–15 HCP, balanced
    2♣: relay (Stayman)
    2◇, 2♡: Jacoby transfer
    2♠: minor-suit Stayman
    2NT, 3NT, 4NT, etc.: quantitative
    3 of a suit: splinter, 4-4-4-1 or 5-4-3-1 distribution, stiff in named suit

4♣: Gerber

4◇, 4♡: Texas transfer (on in competition if there is room to bid 4◇)

4♠: Baron

2♣: 11–15 HCP, ≥ six clubs or ≥ five clubs and a four-card major

2◇: relay

2♡, 2♠: ≥ five-card suit, invitational

2NT: invitational

3♣: to play

3♡, 3♠: natural, forcing

3NT: to play

2◇: 11–15 HCP, 4-4-1-4 or 4-4-0-5

2♡, 2♠, 3♣: to play

2NT: invitational

3◇: relay

> *3♡: minimum*

> *3♠: maximum*

> *3NT: diamond singleton is A, K or Q*

> *4♣: 4-4-0-5*

2X, X = ♡ or ♠: 5–10 HCP, ≥ six-card major

new suit: forcing by unpassed hand

2NT: relay

> *3 of new suit: feature*

> *3X: minimum*

> *3NT: semi-solid suit*

3X, 3NT: to play

2NT: 0–10, 5-5 or longer in the minor suits

3♣, 3◇: to play

3♡: relay

> *3♠: minimum*

> *3NT: maximum*

> *4♣, 4◇: ≥ six-card suit*

3NT: to play

4♣, 4◇, 5♣, 5◇: preemptive

Most balanced hands of ≤ 12 HCP are passed.

Over interference:

Principles of handling interference in a relay auction:

- After interference in front of relayer, in an invitational or game-forcing auction: pass is the relay; DBL or RDBL to play.

- After interference in front of responder, in an invitational or game-forcing auction: pass is neutral, DBL or RDBL descriptive.
- After 1♣, any, pass or negative, and non-pass by fourth hand, pass by opener suggests 16-18 balanced; DBL is takeout; cue is relay.
- After 1♣, interference: twobelows are to play opposite 16-18 balanced; other suit bids are forcing for one round; DBL or RDBL positive.

1♣, then interference:

pass: neutral

twobelow: to play opposite 16–18 balanced

other suit calls: natural, one-round force

cheapest suit bid: relay

DBL or RDBL: positive, game forcing, usually no good suit

cheapest suit bid: relay

Principles of handling interference after opening 1X (X = ♦, ♡ or ♠):
- DBL is negative through 3♠; negative free bids, of course.
- After interference below 1NT, everything is the same (RDBL = 11-13, no fit).
- After interference at or above 1NT, cuebid shows limit raise or big hand, 2NT is natural.

One of a suit, then DBL:

RDBL: 10-13 HCP, no fit; all other calls same as 1X–pass

One of a suit, then overcall:

new suit at one-level: forcing

1NT: relay

all raises: to play

cuebid of suit shown by opposition: forcing raise (flawed, if 2NT was available)

non-jump new suit at two-level, 2NT, or minor at three-level: not forcing

jump to 2NT: limit raise or better, with A , K or Q of trump

jump to 3NT: forcing raise with 2 of the top 3 trumps

non-jump 3NT: to play

1NT, then overcall:
>   2NT: relay to 3♣ (Lebensohl: slow shows stopper)
>   cue: Stayman
>   other: natural, not forcing

Defensive bidding:

Principles of bidding after a takeout double:
- Cheapest response which is not a logical slam, game or twobelow is neutral (the equivalent of passing if RHO had bid). Note that this means certain "jump" responses do not promise the usual 9-11 HCP, but only a desire to bid the suit.
- Cuebids by doubler are relays.

DBL of opening bid: relay (takeout)
>   cheapest response: neutral, unless it is a logical slam, game or twobelow.
>>   For example, all these are neutral responses:
>>   1♡–DBL–pass–1♠, 1♠–DBL–pass–2♣,
>>   2♡–DBL–pass–2NT, 2♠–DBL–pass–2NT.
>>   Exception: 3♡–DBL–pass—3♠ to play, 4♣ neutral.
>   non-jump call: offers to play. This includes, e.g., 1♡–DBL– pass–2♠
>>   which promises no more than 1♡–DBL–2♡–2♠.
>   other: real suit or real desire to play NT (as if RHO had bid).
>>   new suits: strong
>>   cuebid: relay
>>   jump cue: asks for stopper

1NT overcall: 16–18 HCP, system on if next hand passes, doubles artificially or bids 2♣

Defensive cuebids: Michaels (extended)

Over notrump openings: minimum club call is Landy (relay for majors), NT for minors

Over 1♣ or 1♣–pass–1◇, against any big club system: Mathe (DBL for majors, 1NT for minors)

Readers are encouraged to experiment, then send gripes and suggestions to the author (easily found on the web).

DEALS, SESSION 1

Deals not otherwise attributed are constructions of the author.

Board 2 was played by the author, partnered by Alfred Aho, at the Livingston Bridge Club in New Jersey, September, 1993.

Board 4 arose in the Spingold semifinals, in Nashville TN, 2007. As reported by Barry Rigal [15], the Polish star Cezary Balicki played three notrump with our West cards, but a (low) club lead deprived him of the opportunity for a brilliancy.

Board 8 appeared in the Grand National Teams match, in Atlanta GA, January, 1986. North-South held

$$\spadesuit A K Q 5 \quad \heartsuit - \quad \diamond Q 9 8 4 \quad \clubsuit A Q 9 7 3$$

opposite

$$\spadesuit 7 6 4 2 \quad \heartsuit A 8 3 \quad \diamond 6 5 \quad \clubsuit K 6 4 2$$

Your author misplayed the hand by ruffing the heart lead and drawing two rounds of trumps, but made it anyway when the third round of clubs was ruffed by the defense. The following morning he finally figured out how to play the hand correctly and sent it to Jeff Rubens at *The Bridge World,* who published a slightly altered version [16] as "Wolf in Sheep's Clothing."

Board 13 was published by Krysztof Martens [13] and brought to my attention by Chip Martel.

Board 15 was adapted from the author's own article [27].

The remarkable construction given after Board 18, a hand in which any player can make three notrump, was found by John Beasley [1] and published in 1988. Fifteen years later Beasley was amused to see his deal in *The Guardian,* cited as a sensational new computer discovery. Apparently one Thomas Andrews had programmed a computer to search rotationally symmetric deals, and had re-discovered Beasley's creation.

A pair of North-South hands with 40 HCP and only mediocre play for 6NT was constructed by the author and published in *The Bridge World* many years ago.

North

♠ —

♡ —

◇ Q J

♣ K Q J 9 8 7 6 5 4 3 2

▭

South

♠ A K Q J 2

♡ A K Q J 2

◇ A K

♣ A

Note that the diamond-suit duplication is essential. Lengthen dummy's diamond holding and the slam is excellent, because now a defender who has five of one major and three or fewer of the other can be endplayed.

Herbert's "homework" problems and the question of whether there is a deal in which North-South can make seven of any suit but not even 5NT are, as far as the author knows, unsolved.

Board 20 was based on a hand pointed out (generously, after he misplayed it) by Billy Cohen, from the 2004 Cavendish pairs.

The idea for Board 21 came from a deal on p. 228 of Pietro Forquet's excellent book about the Blue Team [8].

Board 22 was contributed by Swedish mathematician Johan Wästlund, who is (justly) famous for having solved the long-open problem of optimal play in two-person, single-suit whist [23, 24].

Board 24 arose in a '60s bridge match between Harvard and MIT, described in [33]. It was your author who went down in three notrump; the defending remark attributed to Corky was made by his partner, Mark Thompson.

The 'fundamental theorem of bridge,' cited by Mildred after Board 25, was familiar to at least some players in the Harvard bridge scene in the '60s. It need hardly be pointed out that if you actually believe six diamonds always makes, you will bid it all the time, and it won't. It's one of those maxims that works only if you *don't* believe it.

The declarer play problem faced by Corky on Board 26 arose in the final session of the Flight A Pairs, at the New York Winter Regional in December 1995. The declarer, bridge columnist Rosalyn Teukolsky, played as Corky did and realized her error, despite the fact that for her the lie of the East-West cards made the hand completely unmakeable.

DINNER

The idea of 'Audit Blackwood,' along with several other conventions for less-than-perfect players, was communicated to the author by Dave Leonard of Atlanta.

In the 1970s, University of Oregon mathematician Matthew L. Ginsburg helped to revolutionize the way computer programs played the hand, by giving up on teaching them the way humans are taught, and instead letting them learn by playing double-dummy against a random sample of opponents' hands. In [9] he also predicted an analagous change in how computers would bid, but, as Herbert points out, this part does not seem to have taken place.

M-Z-M was devised in the '60s by Ed Manfield, Frank Zieve and Cornelius Marx, and promulgated via a voluminous mimeographed summary. It was indeed a well thought-out system, incorporating many then-new ideas.

The cooperative bidding system alluded to by James, which produces a different auction for every deal, was first (as far as we know) published by renowned game theorist Elwyn Berlekamp [5] in 1976; but the existence of such a system was known already to Rand Corporation's Emmett Keeler in 1967. Among later re-discoverers is bridge writer Don Kersey [11].

The diagram on the following page shows how the four players can reveal the location of two specified cards, using only the interval between two consecutive bids (here, 3♢ and 3♡).

Suppose that at this point in the auction the two cards under consideration are the minor-suit nines. The diagram assumes that it is South who, in the process of revealing the locations of the previous two cards, is supposed to bid 3♢. But if South actually has both minor nines, the chart says he skips to 3♡ (or even higher, if he holds the next two cards under consideration as well).

Suppose that North has the ♢9 and East the ♣9. Following the chart, and not having both cards, South bids 3♢; holding neither, West passes. So the left-hand branch of the chart is activated.

North, not having both nines, is instructed to pass. Now East, not having both, has to double. Back to South, who, with neither minor-suit nine, has to redouble. ('X' on the chart signifies a wasted branch, never taken. There are 22 ways to get from 3♢ to 3♡, but only 16 ways the minor nines can be distributed.)

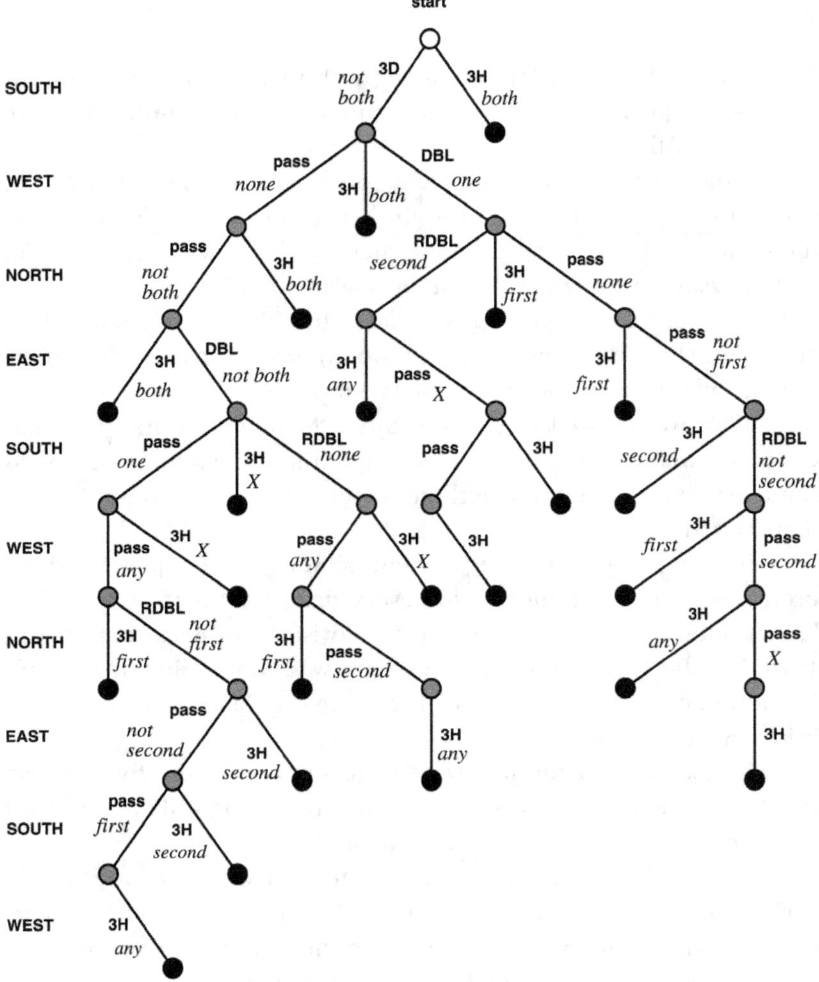

Continuing the example, it's West's turn, and he has no choice: he must pass. North, with the 'first' of the cards in question—the ◇9—is instructed to bid 3♡ (or higher if he has both of the next two cards).

Notice that by the time North gets to bid, South and West have denied holding either minor nine, and North and East have each denied holding both. So, North and East must each have one minor nine, and North's call—pass or bid—settles the question of who has which.

DEALS, SESSION 2

Like Board 24 of Session 1, Board 2 arose in "The Great Charles River Grudge Match" [33] between Harvard and MIT. But there, the big heart hand did not pass over 5◇ doubled, nor attempt to get partner to bid the suit. Thus, the players could only speculate as to whether the spade hand would have made the right inferences.

The successful declarer in the real Board 3 was engineer and bridge ace Apolinary Kowalski, in the international tournament in Deauville, 1992. See pages 71–72 of the highly-recommended volume *The Bridge Magicians* [10].

Boards 5 and 6 are adapted from the author's article [27]. The idea for Board 5 arose in a conversation with Kit Woolsey.

Board 7 is based on a deal [25] constructed by Johan Wästlund, illustrating (as does also the earlier Board 22) his elegant theory of higher-order endplays. Here is another construction of his:

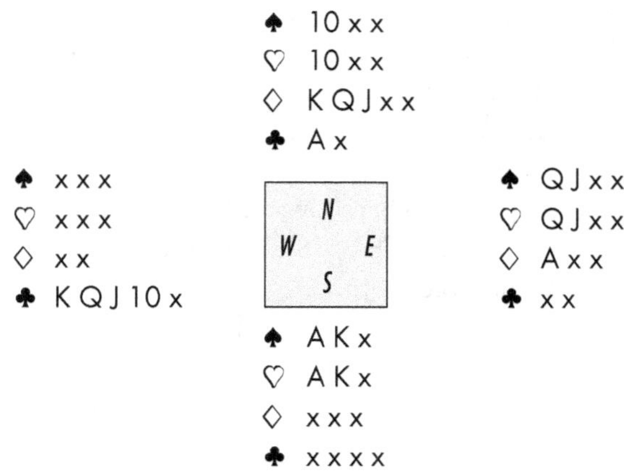

North or South make 3NT on any lead, with the help of a "second-order" throw-in against East.

One example of Tush's fallacious reasoning in Board 8 can be found in [22], where the issue is whether, with

♠8 6 5 4   ♡K Q 9 6 5   ◇J 10 7   ♣3

to make a negative free bid of 2♡ after partner's opening bid of 1◇ is overcalled by 1♠. The writer argues: "You have minimum points and only five mediocre hearts, but your spade length (and partner's presumed shortness) makes it more likely that dummy will have fair support."

Here is a second example, not as egregious, from *The Bridge World* [12], whose editor knows better. In 'Improve Your Bidding,' at matchpoints with no one vulnerable, you hold

♠3 ♡QJ9 ◇KJ8642 ♣532

and it goes 1♣, 1♠, 2♣ to you. Recommended is 3◇ (preemptive): "You are allowed to cut a little off the corner when you have… the hope that partner is short in the opponents' suit (thus not likely too short in yours)."

Board 10 is based on a hand defended by Dutch star Jan Jansma during the Scheveningen Teams, February 1995. Like Tush, Jansma only spotted the killing diamond pitch afterwards.

The North-South hands in Board 11 were taken from [17], where they were (mis)used to make the point that you *shouldn't* rush to draw trump. The lesson began, "One of my closest friends begins the play of each hand by drawing trumps. I once asked him his reason for this habit, and he gave me his answer: 'If a fire should break out, at least I'd have the trumps drawn.' "

Board 12 was played correctly and successfully by Giorgio Belladonna, as reported on p. 66 of [8], in the Roma v. Firenze match of an Italian Teams Championship.

Boards 13 and 14 are adapted from [32].

ACKNOWLEDGMENTS

The author is grateful to his long-suffering bridge partners (Dave Kelly, Matt Franklin, Graham Brightwell and Chris Storm), and his even-more-long-suffering life partner Lois, for their help and forebearance during the development of cryptographic techniques and the Ricochet system. In addition, Franklin, Brightwell and Storm, together with Elwyn Berlekamp, Scot Drysdale, Betty Fleischer, Roy Hughes, Chip Martel, Pinhas Romik, and Johan Wästlund were indispensible in finding errors and room for improvement in the first draft of this book. Any further blunders—and I'm sure there are some—are solely the responsibility of your humble author.

The "double-dummy par" scores in the book, insofar as they are correct, owe a great deal to Bill Bailey's *Deep Finesse* double-dummy analyzer—possibly among the best-written pieces of software ever.

Finally, thanks are due to the founders of the Albert Bradley Third Century Professorship in the Sciences, at Dartmouth. The freedom afforded by this chair has made it possible for the author to devote more time than would otherwise be possible to this and other projects involving mathematical outreach and recreation.

BIBLIOGRAPHY

[1]   Beasley, John. "3NT against any defence." *The Games and Puzzles Journal* 1 (1988): 52 and 68.

[2]   Beaver, Donald; Haber, Stuart; and Winkler, Peter. "On the isolation of a common secret." In *The Mathematics of Paul Erdös* Vol. II, R. L. Graham and J. Nesetril, eds. Springer-Verlag, Berlin, 1996: 121–135.

[3]   Benjamin, Albert. "Suggestions for a new trump signal I–IV." *Bridge Magazine*, December 1976: 344–348, January 1977: 32–26, February 1977: 90–95, April 1977: 227–231.

[4]   Bennett, Deborah J. *Logic Made Easy.* W. W. Norton & Co., 2004.

[5]   Berlekamp, Elwyn. "Cooperative bridge bidding." *IEEE Transactions on Information Theory*, November 1976: 753–756.

[6]   Fisher, Michael J. and Wright, Rebecca N. "Multiparty secret key exchange using a random deal of cards." *Proceedings of CRYPTO 1991.* Springer-Verlag Lecture Notes on Computer Science #576, 1992: 141– 155.

[7]   ———. "Bounds on secret key exchange using a random deal of cards." *Journal of Cryptology* 9, 1996: 71–99.

[8]   Forquet, Pietro. *Bridge with the Blue Team.* Victor Gollancz Ltd, London, 1987.

[9]   Ginsberg, Matthew L. "How computers will play bridge." *The Bridge World* 67 #9 (June 1996): 3–7.

[10]   Horton, Mark and Kielbasinski, Radoslaw. *The Bridge Magicians.* Master Point Press, Toronto, 2001.

[11] Kersey, Don. *The Bridge World online.* Esoterica (undated), http://www.bridgeworld.com/default.asp?d=esoterica&f=perfect.html/.

[12] Kraft, Beverly. "Improve Your Bidding." *The Bridge World* vol. 80 #3, (December 2008): 35–36.

[13] Martens, Krysztof. In *Przeglad Brydzowy* (the official magazine of the Polish Bridge Union). January 1992.

[14] Portmann, Natalie. "How many steps are necessary to separate a bigraph?" *Journal of Combinatorial Theory Series B* 84 #1, 2002: 126–129.

[15] Rigal, Barry. "Music City Spingold." *The Bridge World* 79 #5 (February 2008): 3–19.

[16] (Rubens, Jeff). "Potpourri: Wolf in sheep's clothing." *The Bridge World* 57 #10 (July 1986): 24–25.

[17] Sheinwold, Alfred. *The Pocket Book of Bridge Puzzles*, Number 3. Pocket Books, New York (1970): 95–96.

[18] Simons, John L. "Bridge cryptography fundamentals." *Cryptologia* 30 #3, 2006: 281–286.

[19] Truscott, Alan. "Odd signal switch." *The New York Times*, Sunday, July 13, 1980.

[20] ———. "Help from the defense." *The New York Times*, Sunday, December 28, 1980.

[21] ———. "Encrypted signal has been an advance for the defense." *The New York Times*, Sunday, June 15, 1987.

[22] Walker, Karen. "Bidding matters." *ACBL Bridge Bulletin* (Feb 2005).

[23] Wästlund, Johan. "A solution of two-person single-suit whist." *Electronic Journal of Combinatorics* 12 2005, #R43.
See also: Linkoping Studies in Mathematics No.3, 2005, www.ep.liu.se/ea/lsm/2005/003/.

[24] ———. "Two-person symmetric whist." *Electronic Journal of Combinatorics* 122005, #R44. See also: Linkoping Studies in Mathematics No.4, 2005, www.ep.liu.se/ea/lsm/2005/004/.

[25] ———. "Higher order throw-ins." *The Bridge World* online, Esoterica (2005),
http://www.bridgeworld.com/default.asp?d=esoterica&f=johan.html/.

[26] Winkler, Peter. "Encrypted signaling." *The Bridge World* 51 #7, (April 1980): 25–26.

[27] ———. "Knockout." *The Bridge World* 52 #4 (January 1981): 18–22.

[28] ———. "Cryptologic techniques in bidding and defense, Part I (mathematical theory)." *Bridge Magazine*, April 1981: 148–149. Available online at http://www.blakjak.demon.co.uk/brx_win1.htm/.

[29] ———. "Cryptologic techniques in bidding and defense, Part II (constructive bidding)." *Bridge Magazine* May 1981: 186–187. Available online at http://www.blakjak.demon.co.uk/brx_win2.htm/.

[30] ———. "Cryptologic techniques in bidding and defense, Part III (defensive bidding)." *Bridge Magazine* June 1981: 226–227. Available online at http://www.blakjak.demon.co.uk/brx_win3.htm/.

[31] ———. "Cryptologic techniques in bidding and defense, Part IV (defensive play)." *Bridge Magazine* July 1981: 12–13. Available online at http://www.blakjak.demon.co.uk/brx_win4.htm/.

[32] ———. "My night at the Cryppie Club." *Bridge Magazine* August 1981: 60–63.
Available online at http://math.dartmouth.edu/~pw/cryppie.htm/.

[33] ———. "The great Charles River grudge match." *The Bridge World* 53 #10, (July 1982): 5–7.

[34] ———. "The advent of cryptology in the game of bridge." *Cryptologia* 7 #4, October 1983: 327–332.

Peter Winkler, inventor of cryptologic methods for the game of bridge, is author of nine bridge articles—also two books of mathematical puzzles, a portfolio of compositions for ragtime piano, 135 research papers in mathematics and the theory of computing, and a dozen patents in cryptology, holography, distributed computing, optical networking, and marine navigation. His 'day job' is Professor of Mathematics and Computer Science, and Albert Bradley Third Century Professor in the Sciences, at Dartmouth College, Hanover, New Hampshire.

MASTER POINT PRESS ON THE INTERNET

www.masterpointpress.com

Our main site, with information about our books and software, reviews and more.

www.teachbridge.com

Our site for bridge teachers and students—free downloadable support material for our books, helpful articles, forums and more.

www.bridgeblogging.com

Read and comment on regular articles from MPP authors and other bridge notables.

www.ebooksbridge.com

Purchase downloadable electronic versions of MPP books and software.